SUPER SPORT

RALPH BLAND

Published by Underground Voices
www.undergroundvoices.com
Editor contact: Cetywa Powell
Proofreader: Abbie Waters

ISBN #: 978-0-9988923-0-6
Printed in the United States of America.

SUPER SPORT

Ray Roberts can tell his mother is bent totally out of shape when he walks into the kitchen after getting home from the car lot. Loretta is standing all straight and tense in front of the sink peeling potato after potato like they'd done something to her recently and she's sworn to get even. She doesn't even have her TV turned on over in the corner so she can watch any of the Saturday afternoon country music shows broadcast from WSM in Nashville, even though she always denies paying any actual attention to Porter or Dolly or whoever's show is on. She says she only turns on that TV for the noise that is there, so she can concentrate in the kitchen while she cooks, so that the music drowns out the sounds of lawnmowers and dogs barking and loud cars screeching their tires racing up and down the street like they do lately. She jerks the paring knife with every thrust, all the time looking out the window at Ray's dad out in the back driveway changing the oil on the family car. Ray has seen his dad back there working when he came in, and he thinks their Ford Galaxy must have the cleanest oil in all of Goodlettsville, Tennessee, because there is hardly ever a Saturday Albert Roberts isn't out there doing something to it, changing it, checking it, flushing it, all after working in the Jim Johnson Ford dealership repair shop all week long. Ray figures it is either great diligence on his dad's part or it is just one of those myriad things he routinely does to avoid spending too much time with Loretta inside the house.

"I hope that potato isn't supposed to be a substitute for me because of something I did. I'd be skinned alive by now."

Loretta looks at Ray with her half-smile. Ray's mother is a devout member at Goodlettsville First Church of Christ, so she isn't allowed to totally or absolutely break out into a grin.

"I'm just trying to get dinner ready," she says. "I'm behind."

"Dinner?" he asks. "I didn't think Saturday night was a sit-down dinner night around here. Usually we all go our separate ways and eat somewhere else."

"We're having company tonight," she says. "You were already gone when I found out. Your Uncle Jack is on vacation, and he's driving down from Clarksville to spend some time with his friends in Nashville. I talked him into stopping by on the way in to have dinner with us."

Jack is Loretta's brother, Ray's uncle, but Jack isn't Loretta's favorite person to have come by for dinner and a visit. He is, however, the only member of her side of the family from West Tennessee left to invite over. Loretta's parents—Ray's grandparents on her side—are both long dead, so far dead and buried Ray barely remembers them at all, and her older sister, Dora, has just finished dying of cancer a little over a year ago. Jack, then, is the baby of the family, three years younger than Loretta and five years behind Dora. Loretta still feels a cringe whenever Jack happens to materialize in her presence. She and Dora had been given the job of babysitting Jack from the very beginning long ago, from birth almost, particularly when their father drowned in Dale Hollow Lake on one of his fishing trips. They all had to move to Nashville so Loretta's mother could work graveyard shifts at the Aladdin factory manufacturing lunchboxes and thermos jugs, and the two sisters had been left with the job of watching after Jack. Right from the start Jack had never been an easy one to manage. Even as a grade-schooler he had a way of taxing his sisters and getting on their last nerves.

For one thing, Loretta and Dora always had to watch their little brother like they were hawks. Always. It was never a matter of one sister babysitting while the other got to go and do something else. No, it took both of them just to keep Jack Patterson in check. He was always watching, configuring, plotting and deliberating on what to reach for, what to snatch, where to go and how fast he had to run to get to that place where he already knew he wasn't supposed to go. It wasn't that he was mean and it wasn't that he didn't know right from wrong. It was just that Jack was always going to do what Jack wanted to do. It was that way from the beginning and there wasn't any changing it. He couldn't be told no. It couldn't be beaten out of him. What the sisters learned to do was go with the flow, to somehow beat their little brother to the punch.

Which was hard to do, for Jack was nimble and Jack was quick and Jack was very, very smart.

By the time Jack hit adolescence there weren't many ways to stop him or keep him in check. Dora was a senior in high school by then, busy with her own burgeoning life and preparing to leave the nest to go out on her own, and Loretta was sixteen and a sophomore herself, and although the Depression lagged on and the War had not yet begun, still there was a restlessness in her too as there seemed to be in most everyone else she knew. The feeling that pervaded everyone was that the world was changing and there was something in the wind, and everyone needed to watch and pay attention or they might just get left behind when this big something came by. Loretta had her mind set on other things besides Jack. She was busy watching and waiting with everyone else. She didn't have the time or the inclination to spend all her day dealing with her precocious little brother.

Ray walks away now down the narrow hall to his room. There is an idea festering in his head that has come to him at the mention of his Uncle Jack. Before he takes his shower he stands at the tiny bathroom window and watches his father worry and fret over the Galaxy. Ray has been at work at the used car lot detailing cars for most of this Saturday, but he can recount from tradition and memory all the tasks his father has performed during this day. He has checked both cars mechanically first thing. The Galaxy and the Fairlane he calls his own and never allows anyone else to drive, then, if the oil hasn't needed changing or the radiator flushed or anything else under the hood adjusted or replaced. He has toted out the Hoover from the garage and vacuumed out the previous week's accumulated dirt from both floorboards. After that, both cars got washed and waxed in a professional workmanlike manner, while the Zenith radio from the garage shelf broadcasted baseball and football games and stock car races from places far from their Goodlettsville home, which is mainly out in the country compared to down the road to the capital city of Nashville.

The idea in Ray's head is all about Uncle Jack coming to visit. It hasn't been that long ago—two years at the most—since Uncle Jack had come down from Clarksville and given Ray's older brother John a sizeable amount of cash to put with Albert and Loretta's monetary present for a graduation gift. John had been able to get into a late model Falcon for himself, though Ray remembered how John had actually wanted a Plymouth Fury initially, but had settled for the Falcon in the end, since Albert wasn't about to donate any of his hard-earned pay on anything that didn't emanate from the company line. So it was either John got a Ford product or Al and Loretta's cash gift would dwindle almost to the point of being classified as not much. Maybe John would get a new suit or a watch for graduating or some other consolation prize like that, so the Falcon had won out.

Ray stands under the shower spray thinking of Uncle Jack and how his visits usually go. It doesn't seem to him that his mother likes Jack all that much. It is more like she has to force herself to smile at him when he is around and cook a meal for him and take him into her house for appearances, just so the neighbors and the people she goes to church with won't think it is strange she doesn't want to have much to do with the last remaining member from her side of the family. Ray can sense this attitude from his mother and can almost empathize with his Uncle Jack for it, for he generally feels the same sort of vibration coming from his mother toward him too. He isn't imagining it or making it up in his seventeen year-old brain either. No, it is definitely there. It isn't there for John or his sister Brenda. Sometimes it is there for his dad, but Loretta tries to hide that mostly. But it is definitely there for him, just like it is always there for Uncle Jack.

It isn't that his dad doesn't like Uncle Jack; it is more he does his best not to get too close to him, for fear that nearness in proximity might give some of Jack's aura the chance to rub off on him in some way. It is possible that listening to Jack's stories and jokes and allowing them to seep in, some of that attitude and personality and lack of respect for convention might enter his own being, and Albert Roberts has worked too hard for too many years to allow something wild and unpredictable like that to occur on his watch.

John, too, despite that cash gift his uncle had given him for graduation, is still reluctant to get too close to Jack, and Brenda seems almost frightened of his voice and energy when he is around, as if there is something in her strange uncle ready to devour her before she has the chance to grow up. Most of the time she just looks at him like he is entirely too much, like a frog in her biology class she is observing under a microscope but isn't about to start trying to dissect.

But Ray knew it was him his uncle felt the most comfortable with on his visits. Even when Ray was small there had seemed to be some sort of spark between his uncle and him that was not there for anyone else. Ray would find himself climbing onto Jack's lap while he sat on the sofa in the living room, wrestling with him during meals and conversations, constantly involved in some form of contact and idolization in one way or another, doing his darndest to enter into his uncle's world and station as if there was something contained in that atmosphere that might change and elevate the world he lived in that was not there when Jack was absent.

Out of the shower and dripping wet, it comes to Ray Roberts on this Saturday afternoon, this Palm Sunday Eve in 1967, that the chance and opportunity he's been waiting for and pondering over might possibly be on its way down the highway from Clarksville to his very door right this minute. Ray wonders about this and reminds himself what has always happened in his life when he has maybe counted on something to happen too much and forgot what sometimes transpired when he lets himself want something too much. He tells himself to play it cool this time around.

~~~~~

It isn't like he had an appointment or anything—Jimmy King was going to come by and pick him up and the two of them were going to go out and drive around—but Ray is still impatient for his uncle to arrive and for everyone to get seated for dinner. John was in Knoxville going to school and working at a Food Lion, so he wouldn't be around for this visit, but Brenda has been detained from going off to an early movie, and his parents have mentioned to Ray he needs to stick around for a while too. Ray agreed, not bothering to tell them what he has on his mind and what part Uncle Jack might play in it.

Ray is sitting on the porch swing when he sees Uncle Jack's glossy red Eldorado turn at the corner and come down the street, the top down and the radio blasting Johnny Cash singing "Ring of Fire." With the sun setting, the rays of the spring sun shine on the Cadillac and make it look almost as ablaze and hot as the song playing on the radio. Uncle Jack is behind the wheel, dark sunglasses fitted on his nose and a straw Fedora cocked back on his head. The last time Uncle Jack was here he was beginning to go a little bald. Ray wonders if there is any hair growing under the hat.

Loretta has worked herself thin on this dinner for her brother, and just like always, she is in the midst of asking herself why. This Saturday evening is just like any other evening when it comes to her and Jack—no matter how much she tries to do for him he is still ungrateful and appreciates none of her efforts. This is the way it has always been with him. She can remember giving up evenings and not going out on dates just to make sure he was being taken care of, and generally all she ever received for her good will and concern was Jack playing some awful trick on her—a lizard in her underwear drawer, rummaging through her purse and reading her personal notes, disappearing from the house after bedtime for long extended periods of time, and all the while laughing like a lunatic at her anger and exasperation and flashing that smile that said this time was nothing, sis, you just wait and see what I've got up my sleeve for next time. That's the way it's always been up to now, and on this night she can see it starting all over again.

She watches the way he messes with Albert, always picking at him with that teasing manner, baiting Albert on being a hard worker and a good husband and for trying to bring up his children the right way. She guesses it's a good thing Jack has no children of his own; if he did she supposed they'd just be allowed to run wild and do whatever they wanted to do. She's never worried about the way he acts around John too much. Thank God John has a level head on his shoulders and doesn't fall for all the malarkey that comes out of his uncle's mouth. John is like Albert, in the fact he just nods his head and tries to keep his distance in a polite sort of way. Brenda is only thirteen, but she already knows what kind of trouble her Uncle Jack is. Loretta can see Brenda trying to not even be in the same room as Jack, and Loretta is happy about that and can't blame Brenda for being this way one little bit. She just wonders when the time is finally going to come when Albert gets tired of getting teased about everything under the sun, about being a good man and being loyal to his company and his church and his family and finally just doubles up his fist and knocks some sense and respect into his brother-in-law, but Loretta knows that's not going to happen. Albert is a big man, not afraid of anybody, but she doubts he could do much with Jack when it came to a fight. Jack is a big man too, and he knows a whole lot about fighting. He'd been in fights all his life, all the way from the time he started school. The thing of it was he was not just in a lot of fights, but he liked it. He liked a fight like he likes drinking and easy women and his big red flashy Cadillac.

What infuriates and worries her the most, though, is the way Ray sidles up to his uncle every time he comes by, the way he looks at Jack and almost acts like he wants to imitate him in his actions and his speech. If Loretta could just put a finger on this budding idolatry she'd tear into Ray and let him know she wasn't going to have any part of it while he is living under her roof, but so far nothing has ever really happened to prove her suspicions. Maybe it isn't true and she is just imagining this attraction between Jack and her son, but—like it was with a lot of things concerning her brother—it certainly does bear watching. She's seen Jack weave his spell on others before. Why, she had one of her best friend's younger sister get all wound up with Jack in high school and almost have to drop out of classes just to get over it. And that wasn't the only time either. She could go on and on with stories of some of the things Jack Patterson had done.

So she's angry with Jack already, and he's only been around ten minutes at the most. She thinks about this fact and wonders if she is being unreasonable, but just a moment's mental recounting of her past experiences with her brother resolves her of any blame or guilt about her feelings. He's lucky, she thinks, that all she is angry. He's lucky she hasn't taken out Albert's hunting rifle and shot him already. She's been that perturbed at him for as long as she can recall.

There are fried pork chops, mashed potatoes, fresh green beans, and corn on the cob. She's put together a nice tossed salad and has a whole pan of cornbread. There's a choice of sweet or unsweetened iced tea, and an apple pie sits over on the counter for dessert. She even went to the Piggly Wiggly and bought two flavors of their most expensive ice cream. Why, she doesn't really know. It's not like she is trying to impress Jack or feels like she owes him such a good meal for anything. If anything, it ought to be the other way around. Jack should be doing something nice for her. She thinks of all the meals she's made him, how many times she's done his laundry down through the years. He should be the one treating her. But then she thinks about the time he helped out on the mortgage when Albert was out of work with a broken arm. She thinks about the money he gave John for graduation to get a car. It was a lot. Jack didn't have to be that generous. And he'd never let Albert pay him back either, so maybe Jack was treating her in his own way, Loretta and all the members of her family.

Of course, Jack is a bachelor, and he has a good-paying job. He'd bought himself that Cadillac just like that, so it wasn't like he didn't have money to burn. But still, he didn't have to help them out like he has, so maybe Loretta shouldn't be so mad at him all the time.

She can see the look on Albert's and the children's faces when they notice she's let out the leaf on the dining room table and covered it with one of her best cloths. Usually the dining room table is reserved for Thanksgiving and Christmas and Easter, so for it to be adorned this way on a Saturday night a week ahead of a major holiday is something different indeed.

"Boy," Ray says, "you must really rate, Uncle Jack. We wouldn't get this fancy even if President Johnson and Ladye Bird were coming by."

"This is pretty special," Jack says. "You've outdone yourself again, Loretta. I'm not so sure I know how to act. I'm used to getting all my food on a paper plate down at the Foxhole Bar and Grill in Clarksville."

Albert starts into a prayer and Ray looks down at his empty plate with his eyes open, making sure nobody can see they aren't closed. He can't help but take a quick glance at his uncle to see if he is cheating on the prayer too. He seems to have his eyes closed, but Ray doesn't truly think it is in prayer. It is more like he is taking a little siesta. Jack's eyes may be tired from driving. But then, Jack is a bus driver, so he drives long stretches of road all the time. The trip down from Clarksville wasn't going to tire him out that much.

"Amen," Albert says.

"Well, Jack," Albert says as the dishes are going around, "have you been driving to any new places lately, or are you set into the same runs all the time?" Albert is doing his best to be a conversationalist, like his taking the lead is going to keep Jack from bringing something up Albert really doesn't want his kids hearing. Jack likes talking about his personal life too much. There was always some mention of bars and whiskey and such. Women. Albert doesn't much care to hear it himself, but especially not his kids, even if he does have to admit that the stories are usually pretty funny. That Jack could get himself into some real predicaments, that was for sure. And he did know how to tell a good story. He ought to be on television with some of the tales he told.

"I try to mix it up as much as I can," Jack says. "I don't like to get into a rut. I've got so much seniority now I get to pick and choose my runs almost all the time. Sometimes I'll go north to Chicago and Indianapolis and even all the way to New York City, but I only do that in the summertime so I don't have to mess with driving in all that snow. Some of them places I get a good layover and I can see a ballgame or something, maybe even go out on the town." He stops here to wiggle his eyebrows at Ray and smile Albert's way. "If I get into town early enough I can always find me a hot date for the evening. You ever been to Chicago, Albert? There's always something going on in Chi-Town."

"I was in Chicago once," Loretta says. "I went there with Dora when she was going to a convention. That was when she was teaching school. We drove up there and stayed at a motel right outside of town, and she took a bus into town three mornings in a row with a bunch of other teachers staying at the same place. It was summertime. I rode in one morning with them on a Friday and went downtown all day. They had a lot of stores and I almost got lost."

"I like Chicago just fine," Jack says, "but I'll take Miami over it anytime. I like to make that Florida run. The weather's fine and there's plenty of places to go and lots to do. You can go to the Keys if you want. I like to go to the dog track myself."

The conversation goes on like that, Jack talking about all the places he's been between bites and Loretta and Albert trying to keep the subjects somewhere near tame and not fettered and dripping with Jack's descriptions of the slightly lurid borderline sleazy places and locales he's gone and frequented. Ray sits quietly chewing and sipping and digesting both the food and the details Uncle Jack offers, and after a few minutes he decides that it seems to him his uncle has more money coming from his job with Trailways than he knows what to do with. There is the big red Cadillac Eldorado parked outside in the driveway, there are the women and the bars and the gambling joints in all the cities he visits, and there is still always more than enough—it seems to Ray—for Jack to be able to bestow a cash visitation on his older sister and her family. Ray has watched his dad go to work each and every day since he's been a little kid, but he hasn't seen anything of his dad going to hot towns and having fun from all his steadfastness and efforts. All Ray sees is the day in, day out stuff, the going to work and the coming home and the working on the cars on the weekend and going to church and repeating the process every week. He sees his mother worry about the house and John and Brenda and look at him like maybe she might worry about him too, someday maybe, but then it is back to the house and the rest of the family and the church. God, Ray thinks, don't forget the church.

He sees a lot from his vantage point, but what he doesn't see is anybody having too much fun. He doesn't see anybody smiling much. He especially doesn't see anyone with a whole lot of extra cash. He is at the stage where he knows if he has enough money he won't have to worry about not being able to smile. It will come natural to him. All he has to do to be sure of that is to take a good long look at Uncle Jack.

Uncle Jack always has that smile on his face.

Jack could certainly eat. Loretta watches him put away three big pork chops, have double servings of everything, swill down three glasses of sweet tea and polish off two pieces of pie with a city of ice cream on top. How he is able to get out of his chair she doesn't know, but she appreciates the fact that he doesn't light his cigarette there at the table but goes outside on the porch to smoke. Albert smokes too, and it would be good for him to follow Jack's lead and go outside too. As it is he just lights up at the table and anywhere else he wants in the house. After all these years every room smells like smoke, even though it's been so long Loretta truly can't smell anything anymore.

"Your mother says you've been working pretty regularly," Jack says to Ray, who has followed him outside. "What are you doing with all your money? I hope you're not one of these level-headed fellows who tries to save every penny he makes. When I was your age I had so many girlfriends I couldn't make enough money to spend on all of them."

"I don't have a girlfriend to spend money on," Ray says. "A guy's got to have a car before he can get himself a girl. The girls I know like to go places. They don't like to walk."

"What kind of car do you want?" Jack studies the tip of his cigarette and adjusts some tobacco back inside the paper. "I imagine you want one of those four in the floor jobs with the mag wheels and the big engine."

"Not really." Ray looks around to make sure his dad isn't somewhere listening. "I could go with something small myself. I don't even mind if it's an automatic, long as it's not a Ford."

"What's wrong with a Ford?"

"Nothing, I guess, except if I got one Dad would always be telling me what I needed to do with it next."

"You might have something there," says Jack.

"Well, I've got to go, Uncle Jack," Ray says. "I don't have a car and I don't have a date but I do have something to do tonight. A friend of mine is coming by to pick me up. We may go to a movie or something. Probably we'll just ride around a while. He's got his mother's Volkswagen. If I give him a dollar we can ride around all night."

"A dollar in the Eldorado might get you up to the stop sign," Jack smiles.

He watches Ray go down the walk to the front of the driveway, where his friend in his mother's bug has just pulled in to pick him up. The VW is light blue and already beginning to rust, but Jack knows it doesn't matter. He knows it will probably run at least another fifteen years, maybe even forever.

"Why don't you come inside and sit down a while," Loretta asks him. "We're not doing anything except watching a little television. Albert will have to go out into that garage of his in a while and tune in a baseball game or something. He says he gets better reception out there, but I don't know. You and I can catch up a little. I've been wondering what you've been up to lately. All I know about you lately is you're still driving a big old bus for money and a Cadillac for fun. I'm wondering if you've got something going on in between."

"I'm on the road too many hours to have too much going on. I'll be gone a week sometimes. Then back a day or two and I'm gone again. I don't turn any routes down. You start getting picky with Trailways and the first thing you know you're out of work. There's plenty other drivers who'll take a job if you don't. You tell them no and the first thing you know they're calling somebody else instead of you next time."

"Still," Loretta says, "I don't see why you want to work all the time. Seems to me you might want to slow down some and do something else. You've been working like this for a long time."

"You still don't know me that well," Jack grinned. "If you did you'd know it's when I'm not out on the road driving that's the time I start getting myself into trouble. You don't know the least of it."

"You need to settle down," Loretta tells him. "You're getting too old for all that sort of foolishness."

Jack just stands there smiling at her like he always does, knowing how when he does this it really gets under his sister's skin.

He makes himself hang around for almost forty-five minutes before he starts trying to get out the door. He can tell Albert's more than ready for him to go by the way his brother-in-law has some semblance of a smile plastered on his face, because Albert never truly smiles at anything. Nothing pleases him that much. Loretta keeps wanting to drag out pictures of Jack and her and Dora and their momma and daddy from way back when, pictures Jack has seen more than a thousand times and would be happy never to view again, but he makes himself look at them anyway so Loretta won't get any madder at him than she generally is. This, he tells himself, is what family is all about. You have to have a sense of history and step out of yourself a little just so you can see where the people who knew you then and came from the same place you did are in relation to you, just so you get the feeling you're not all alone in the world. He's trying to keep some contact with Loretta and her family, since she's all the family he's got left. He doesn't remember his parents, and Dora is scarcely in his memory anymore. If he doesn't see her picture every now and then he can't visualize her in his mind at all.

That's why two or three times a year he makes the trip down from Clarksville to check in with Loretta and not be so distant. He knows Loretta and he are different as day and night, and he knows she's communicated it to her family by her actions and her words that her brother is a little bit strange, a little bit dangerous and wild. Jack can see it in the eyes of Albert and Brenda and John, even though he's tried to make them like him with some well-timed money here and there. He's spent a few years now making an effort to win himself over to them. He's not so sure it's been worth it or not.

So it's difficult sometimes. It's strained, to say the least. But he knows he hasn't struck out totally with this trying to fit in as an uncle and a brother and all that. He thinks of Ray, gone off down the road now in his friend's mother's Volkswagen. He says goodbye to Loretta and Albert and goes out and gets in his car, ready to ride down the pike toward Nashville. Ray's like you, his brain says. He's the one who likes to see you come around.

But I'd better be careful what I say and do with that boy, Jack thinks. He might be too much like me to not keep an eye on him.

~~~~~

At one time or another on a Friday or a Saturday night, every kid who lives in Goodlettsville or the neighboring towns of Ridgetop or Greenbrier cruises either Bud's Dairy Dip or the Burger Chef around the town square at least once before giving it up for small potatoes and driving in ten miles to Nashville to circle the Shoney's drive-in six or seven times. Whether or not the drivers and their passengers stop and order anything to eat or not is debatable, since most of their funds are invested in gasoline at the beginning of the evening, but it doesn't cost a thing to look at who is parked in the stalls and who is in the cars lined up ahead and behind. In Nashville there are always more kids, more variety from all the big high schools inside the metropolitan city limits. The possibilities are slim anything too exciting is going to happen—Ray hasn't known of anybody from Goodlettsville or anywhere else who's met a new girl or found somebody new to date by motoring in to Nashville to cruise the drive-ins at night—but at least there are new faces and the fleeting chance of romantic intrigue hanging in the air, even if the odds are a million to one.

"I wish you'd stop chain-smoking for at least ten minutes," Ray tells Jimmy King, who is steering the Volkswagen with one hand while lighting a Winston with the other. Jimmy is having trouble doing both things at once, since he has to use a match for his cigarette because the lighter in the VW is burnt out, and the matchbook is a little wet from the Pepsi he's spilled on the seat from when he took his first swig and tried to swallow too much. "Every damned time I go out with you I come home smelling like smoke and get accused of smoking by my mother. I have to go through this whole lecture every single time she does the laundry."

"Why don't you do your own damn laundry?" Jimmy says. "Or you could always take it to the dry cleaners. They don't charge that much. Hell, you're a working man. You can afford it."

"How about you pay for it then, smart ass, since it's your fault I smell like a goddamn chimney all the time? It would be like the bargain price you paid for having the pleasure of my company every Saturday night."

Ray looks out his side window and sees nothing worth feasting his eyes upon. If the girls are good-looking they are already with other guys. They are in Chevys with new paint jobs and Fords with mag wheels and Pontiacs with four speeds, cars with radios and tape players and deep-throated mufflers that make windows rattle when they pass. Ray knows all about these cars. He has experienced a good percentage of them up close and personal, since he is the fellow who cleans and waxes and polishes them up afternoons after school and all day Saturday down at Reed's Used Cars on Main Street, then gets to watch as the boys and their fathers come in and buy them and drive them away. Ray wants to be one of those guys who drive one of those cars away, but he doesn't have the dough for it yet. He is trying, but it is still going to be a while. Unless things change he isn't going to be driving anything home anytime soon.

But he's working on it.

"You know, this scene we're looking at is really beautiful and enchanting," Ray says, "but I've got to tell you I'm getting a little tired and bored with it. Why don't we vamoose out of here and see if we can come up with something to drink besides Pepsis and milkshakes tonight?"

Ray directs Jimmy back out the pike toward Goodlettsville again. They pass through the square on Main and travel through the sparse downtown district, past the Super Saver Grocery and the Morrison Funeral Home and on out the highway to the city limit. They pull over at a liquor store and sit in the car for a minute with Jimmy looking at Ray wondering what kind of plan he has in his head to have him pull over here. Jimmy knows he's never going to pass for twenty-one inside, and he's pretty sure Ray doesn't look any older than him. Ray sits looking out the windshield. The Animals are singing "Bring It On Home To Me" on the radio, and Ray takes his hand and turns the volume down a little.

"I halfway know a guy who works here," he says. "I detailed his Bonneville for him a couple of weeks ago. That's it sitting over there at the side." Ray studies the lot and sees no one else around. "I gave him a good deal on what I did and he was real grateful, said to let him know if I ever needed anything. I figure we can sit out here and wait for somebody to come along and see if they'll buy us a bottle if we paid them, or I can go inside and see if the guy will sell something to me as a favor." Ray looks around again. Goodlettsville is deserted. It's nine o'clock on a Saturday night and everybody's home watching television. "If we wait for somebody to come we'll be here all night. Screw it. It's worth a try. You wait here."

Ray walks in and immediately knows he's out of luck. There's another man standing beside the cash register while the Bonneville owner is restocking the refrigerated wine. He and the cashier look at Ray, and Ray raises his hand.

"Hey," he says. "I was driving by and saw your car outside. I thought I'd stop and say hi."

He stands at the door and grins like an idiot, scanning the store with all its liquor he will never get to drink. The shelves are full, promising him great happiness if he will only draw near.

"Well," he says, "I've got to go. Somebody's waiting on me."

He pushes out the door, already hating having to get back in Jimmy's car with nothing to drink, when he sees his uncle's red Eldorado pull into the lot. Uncle Jack turns off the ignition and gets out, peering at Ray the entire time.

"Fancy meeting you here," he says. "I don't guess I need to ask what you're doing at this place."

"I'm not going to lie to you," Ray smiles. "You probably know what I'm doing here, so I'm just going to go ahead and ask you a favor. I'm wondering if you can help me out. If you can't, just say no and it's all right. I'd just appreciate it if you wouldn't tell on me, that's all."

"Let me guess, buddy. You need a little something from inside that building there, am I right?"

"We want to get something to mix with our cold drinks. Maybe some bourbon, I don't know."

"Or some gin or scotch or vodka or anything else that might do the trick," Jack adds. "Maybe even some of that rot-gut wine that the winos drink down by the railroad tracks—that would be just fine too. Isn't that right?"

Ray stands there grinning. He doesn't quite know how to answer.

"What you're saying is you and your buddy are looking for something you can get drunk on in a hurry, am I right? Tell me if I'm on the right track on this."

"Yes, sir, it's like you're awful close to reading my mind right now. We're sort of looking to maybe do something different tonight. It's Easter vacation and we're out of school," he says, like that counts for something.

"You know your mother would never forgive me for doing something like this, don't you? Hell, your daddy would probably shoot me. He's been looking for a good reason for a while now, and this would for damn sure qualify. That's if he finds out, you know. I'm sincerely hoping that doesn't happen. And as far as your mother never forgiving me, I guess this would be just one more thing on that long list of stuff I've done that she's already got written down in her head. So I guess one more thing isn't going to make that much of a difference."

"I'll give you some money," Ray says.

This makes Jack laugh.

"You don't have to give me money, Ray. Half of the reason I've come down here was to see if I could help any of my family out. I make more money than I can spend. I may as well spend some of it right now in the interests of mankind. I'll go in here and invest in some Jack Daniel's as a graduation gift a year in advance for you. It'll finally be a present one of my kin can truly appreciate. Later on in your life, when you're getting to be an old fart like me, you'll probably look back on this night as the beginning of when the door of earthly pleasures first swung open for you. This night and the first night you're with a girl—that's what you'll remember."

Jack looks at his nephew again, as if he's considering if what he's fixing to do is the right thing or not. He thinks for a minute of when he was seventeen like Ray, when everything was out there and he had to try every trick in the book just to get his hands on the least part of it.

"Go sit in the car," he tells Ray. "I'll be right back."

~~~~~

Jack is back inside of five minutes, but to Ray, waiting with Jimmy inside the car in the lot, it seems like closer to an hour. Ray tries to sit and be cool and listen to whatever song comes on the radio, but he can't help wondering if Uncle Jack is inside the liquor store using their phone to call Loretta and Albert and have them come down here so they can witness what their middle child is attempting to get his uncle to do for him. Ray knows that isn't the case and that Uncle Jack would never do anything to get him in trouble with his folks, but he still can't help not trusting anyone the slightest bit older than him right now. Or younger either, like Brenda, who would tell on him for anything at the drop of a hat. As a matter of fact he could group his friends into that untrustworthy category too, even dumbass Jimmy sitting here beside him, who is his partner in crime for this endeavor tonight. Ray knows that if the going got tough and push came to shove Jimmy would squeal long and hard and waste no time pointing the finger of accusation directly at him.

But the door does open presently and Jack does appear with a paper bag under his arm. Ray doesn't want to act like he is over-anxious or anything, so he makes himself sit still in the seat and not bolt out of the car like what Jack has inside the bag is the answer to all his problems and miseries and needs to be latched onto without any further hesitation. He still has a five dollar bill rolled up in his palm and is in a quandary whether he should force Uncle Jack to take it or not. He doesn't want to appear like a cheapskate or something. It is already bad enough that he is having to enlist someone—especially his close kin—to buy him alcohol because he isn't old enough to do it himself, even though he knows without a doubt he is old enough to drink and get himself as far away from his sorry status as a boy not old enough or experienced enough to take complete care of himself in this rough and tumble life. Ray could write a book on how badly he wants to be gone from the life he is living in the present and how fast he wants to be launched into the future, where there isn't a curfew and he eats what he wants when he wants to and when he wants to go somewhere he has the means to do that too, because there would be a car parked right where he'd left it when he'd gone off somewhere, and it would be sitting there waiting for when he sticks his key in its ignition and gets ready to go somewhere again, which will be a place where he takes care of himself and doesn't have to ask anybody for anything.

"They only had one bottle of Jack Daniel's left, and I'm sorry as can be, buddy boy, but that one was for me. I got you some Jameson's Irish instead, so it isn't like you're settling for rotgut or anything." Jack turns and looks back at the building he's just left. "I can't imagine how any upstanding business owner can allow himself to run out of Jack Daniel's on a Saturday night. This guy either hasn't got any idea what he's doing or the rubes living around here all drink just any old thing like there ain't any tomorrow."

He reaches in the bag and draws forth a green bottle with a gold cap. Across the bottom label Ray can see the word IMPORTED emblazoned in a box.

"This is from Ireland," Jack smiles, "far across the sea. Drink a little bit of this and in a matter of minutes you'll think you're over there yourself."

"I ain't ever had anything like this before," Ray says. "What do you do with it? Can you mix it with something or do you just drink it straight?"

"I guess you can do whatever you want as long as you can swallow it. All I can say is you don't want to get carried away, because this stuff can get rough if you don't watch it. You're not going to be riding around like a couple of fools swigging this stuff, are you?" Jack looks inside the car at the faces of the two boys. "If you fellows don't have somewhere to go where you can light and not have to worry about running into somebody or running off the road I'm not going to let you have this. I'll keep it myself and let you go on somewhere else. Heck, where I'm headed tonight another bottle of booze will be greatly appreciated."

"We're just going to go over to Jimmy's house," Ray says quickly. "His parents are out of town and we're going to sit out on the patio and listen to the radio. I'm not even planning on coming home tonight, and if I do all I have to do is walk. Jimmy doesn't live but about a half a mile away."

"Okay then." Jack looks at the boys one last time, making sure his nephew isn't just shooting him a line and telling him what he wants to hear, which Ray is doing on both counts. "I might see you tomorrow afternoon," he tells Ray. "Your mother wanted me to go to church but I

told her it started too early for me. I told her I might be by
later in the day if I could walk or if I wasn't busy with a
woman. I'm really hoping against hope you don't see my
smiling face tomorrow." He winks at Ray and smiles his
smile again. "Anyway," he says, "be careful, guys."

Ray and Jimmy watch Jack walk over to the Cadillac
and pull away before they take off back down the highway
toward Nashville again. Ray is already breaking the seal and
sticking his nose close to the neck of the bottle so he can
sniff what form of magic potion is inside. It is a raw smell, a
vicious but happy sensation that tickles his nostrils and
wafts up to his eyes. It is all no nonsense and take no
prisoners in this first sniff, and Ray peers into the darkness
of the bottle and wonders what devil might be lurking down
there.

"That was pretty smart of you saying my folks were
out of town," Jimmy says. "I wouldn't have thought of
anything that quick and your uncle would have probably not
let us have anything because of it. You're a better liar than I
am."

"I get a lot of practice," Ray says. "If I told people
the truth I'd never have any fun at all."

He's looked and smelled and imagined what's inside
the bottle enough. Now he has to know what he's dealing
with for sure, so he takes a tentative swallow and swishes
the whiskey around in his mouth. He instantly knows he's
taken too much into his mouth, but he's not going to spit it
out no matter how much it burns. His tongue feels on fire
and the roof of his mouth is acting like there's a dragon
breathing in there. When he swallows there's an explosion
in his throat that goes all the way down like a depth charge
to his belly, and his eyes water over like the ocean racing in
at high tide to pound the shore where his unsuspecting
brain was only a heartbeat ago completely dry. It is like his
brain is being burned by a torch and smacked by one hell of
a wave at the same time. It is such a jolt and a scare like he

has never felt before that he raises the bottle to his lips and takes a second drink—one even larger than the first—again. Wowee, he thinks. Holy Shit.

"Where do you want to go?" Jimmy asks. "Make it somewhere I can park so I can have a little of what you're drinking before it's all gone."

"Go towards downtown," Ray says. "We can park the car at one of the open lots and walk around for a while. You might want to stop and get you a soft drink or something to mix this with. I don't know if you want to try and drink it straight."

"What are you going to do?"

"I'm just going to drink it like this, right from the bottle. I'm afraid all that sugar and carbonation will make me puke."

"Well wait until I get parked, then. I don't want you puking in my mother's car."

They park the car on a back street just down from the jail. There is a bonding company across the way with two guys standing on the porch smoking cigarettes, looking like they are puzzled they aren't so busy on a Saturday night. Ray can't tell if they are looking at him and Jimmy or not, but he starts walking the opposite way so he won't have to talk to them.

"I'm going to head down to Printers' Alley," he tells Jimmy. "It's a bunch of night clubs and strip joints. There's no way we'll ever be able to get in but we can at least watch what people are doing while we're drinking. I'll bet all the cops will be inside watching the shows. They won't be worrying about what we're doing outside."

"Seems to me we ought to be heading in the opposite direction from where there's cops." Jimmy says.

"We go in the opposite direction we ain't going to see anything. Ain't nothing out the other way but winos and queers. At least back this way we might see a girl or two."

"How do you know that? You haven't ever been there before."

"I read the newspapers. I watch TV. I've been meaning to check this place out when I got the chance. I'm not like you. You're ignorant and proud of it. You want to be a dumbass forever. It's like your life goal. I can see you going off to school and majoring in being a dumbass."

"Screw you, Ray. If you get me in trouble tonight you can bet I'll whip your ass the first chance I get."

"Follow me, dumb butt. I'm fixing to take you on a little adventure."

In all honesty Ray has no idea what he is doing or fixing to walk into. Sure, he's read about the clubs in downtown Nashville and heard about how strippers come and go in Printers' Alley almost all the time, but he doesn't know what might happen if he and Jimmy were to come across some woman with no clothes on. He likes to act like he's been around a little bit, like he isn't altogether unfamiliar with alcohol and scantily-dressed females and things that go on in the dead of night in the heart of the city while the town of Goodlettsville is fast asleep fifteen miles up the road; but the truth of it is that what he knows he's seen on TV is a show and he's just taken it from the script and applied it to the real life he figured was happening just beyond his vision and barely out of his reach. The thing of it is he is never going to know about any of it for certain until he goes out and sees it and touches it himself. He knows nobody can tell you these things. He knows you have to see for yourself.

A Krystal restaurant is open on Church Street, so Ray waits outside on the walk while Jimmy goes inside to get a Coke. There are plenty of people walking around downtown, coming out of movies or climbing the hill from the Ryman Auditorium on Broadway after the Grand Ole Opry's first show is over. The department stores are closed, but men hang out under the awnings, smoking cigarettes and drinking from hidden bottles and watching pedestrians pass by and cars go up and down with the faces inside that watch them back.

Ray is carrying the bottle under his shirt so it won't be spotted, tucked inside his pants with his belt supporting it. He wears his sport shirt not tucked in so it can hide the bulge underneath, and he is trying to walk in a natural way so it won't be so obvious he is trying to smuggle something with him that he isn't supposed to have. He is leaning against the corner at a crosswalk with his hands in his pocket looking up at the sky like he doesn't have a worry in the world. He wishes like hell Jimmy would hurry up.

From the alley that runs down the hill a man and a woman come walking toward him. They aren't that easy to ignore, since their arms are intertwined and the man is singing "Oh, Lonesome Me" at the top of his lungs and the woman is laughing so loud she is almost drowning him out. Ray tries to keep from making eye contact, but the woman smiles at him while the man keeps singing and hooks her arm through his so that now he is a part of a trio.

"Hello, baby doll," she says. "How come a dreamboat like you is standing out here in the middle of downtown all alone on a Saturday night?"

If he had been in his right mind Ray would have pulled his arm back and got away from these two as fast as he could, but he's had Jameson's Irish Whiskey taken to such an extent that the danger of this encounter doesn't seem as dire as it might have appeared earlier in the evening, and the woman with her arm hooked through his with her bleached hair and her red dress and her red pumps appears to be a lot more attractive to him than she might have at any other point in his life up till now. So he thinks it is perhaps maybe all right to promenade a few steps up the walk with his new friends, especially with the way the woman leans her body against him in a manner a woman's body has never leaned against him before.

During the sashay her elbow brushes against the bottle hidden beneath his shirt and he knows she's felt what is tucked away there but hopes she is far enough along in her earlier revels that this discovery might be one of those things that don't seem important enough for her to bring up.

"Hey, Clifford," she says, "our new buddy here has a bottle under his shirt. I'll bet you he's just dying to share it with us."

Ray is attempting to disengage and break away from her grasp, but as he tries to separate his arm he feels the bottle make a sickening shift and escape from his belt. He does his best to make a last gasp catch, but the bottle squirts through his fingers and rises eye level to him like an intercontinental ballistic missile and begins its descent before his reflexes can recover enough to make a stab for it. In the sweep of two seconds on his Timex the bottle crashes against the concrete walk and explodes in high octane proof on the side of the building and his shoes. Ray looks down at the liquid soaking into the walk and up at Jimmy who has just emerged from the Krystal with his drink to go and around at the faces of strangers who stop to watch what is going on there on the sidewalk in front of them.

"Aw, honey, I'm awful sorry," the red-shoed floozy in the red dress says. "I didn't know you were so fumbly-fingered."

The man beside her has stopped singing and is laughing now. Ray looks at him and doubles up his fists. He has never hit a grown man before—hell, he's never hit anybody—but it seems like the thing to do now. But Jimmy has his arm now and is pulling him away.

"Come on, man," Jimmy says. "We've got to get the hell out of here."

Ray looks at the broken bottle and its contents soaking into the concrete. Like most of his life lately, this night isn't working out the way he'd planned it.

~~~~~

If Ray had his way his entire family would be heathens. That way they'd all be easier to get along with; but this was one of those things that wasn't going to happen in his lifetime. Sometimes he wondered what kind of rotten luck he was the recipient of that had placed him right in the middle of a devout steadfast Church of Christ household, seeing how his brother and sister seemed to be more than content to be included in the rank and file of that religious faith, and his mother couldn't separate herself from the doctrine for any amount of time whatsoever either, not to go to a movie or to watch television or go on vacation or anything. Heck, all he could remember growing up was when the family went on their yearly summer vacation together they always had to stop whatever they were doing—fishing, swimming, picnicking—to find a Church of Christ congregation somewhere in the vicinity of their cabin or motel room and take valuable time on Sunday mornings to go to some alien church as visitors and hear some strange preacher recite a sermon, then have to shake hands with a bunch of people he'd never seen before and never would see again before they could go back to the vacation part of the week and maybe have a little fun if it could be done in a good Church of Christ type of way.

The only other member of his family who might be the slightest bit like him was possibly his dad, though Ray was uncertain if this was so or not. Albert sometimes seemed a trifle sad or irritated when the burden of church-related events began to mount and monopolize his time, but Ray noticed how his father always managed to adjust and make the best of the situation without a flare-up, which would have resulted in bad relations with Loretta. The way Ray had it figured was Albert was okay most of the time with the church and the whole magilla of rules and regulations as long as it didn't deter him from fishing and hunting and performing car maintenance on the family automobiles on Saturday afternoons with his garage radio drowning out all other forms of life. He would go to a certain point to keep Loretta happy and his family firmly within the Carmelite guidelines, but there was a limit and he made certain he upheld it.

Ray was about ten when he decided he didn't much relish this going to church every time the doors got opened; but being that he was ten and had learned by that time as the middle child in the family that his place was to keep his trap shut and let his older brother get adored by his mother and dad and his younger sister get pampered and be the baby of the family while he as the in-between got to go mainly ignored and unnoticed, which may have been a problem to most middle children in most families but was just fine with him from the very first get-go. It had not taken too much time at all for him to figure out that anonymity and a lack of attention were just the sort of things that would serve him well in the years to come. He learned to say yes and nod in agreement and to never raise a word of dissent. He learned to keep quiet and polite and go along his own way doing what he had planned on doing in the first place, doing it to his own content so long as no one found out about it while he was in the act.

Such is his mindset on Palm Sunday morning, sitting off to the side on the last row of the sanctuary by himself, mentally transported to somewhere else in the galaxy other than where he is, tied to this place only by the view he has of Teresa Mitchell's neck three rows in front of him, the only bare flesh he can see of her, which the sight of makes the baser portion of his mind go into low gutter mode, since all he can concentrate on now in the part of him that remains in this real world is a sense of wonder regarding how Teresa Mitchell might appear naked. This is one of those big questions he has pondered for a while, and he is still in the stages of figuring out how he is going to answer this question. The logical solution would be to ask Teresa out on a date and attempt to charm her out of her wardrobe through food and movies and miniature golf, but the thing of it is Ray doesn't really like Teresa all that much outside of the conjecturing over her unclad form, so it hardly seems worth all the money and time and effort just for what might be a disappointing encounter. It's not just naked Teresa or any other girl without clothes or pretty much anything else in the world he feels he is supposed to pursue; Ray feels this way about most of the pageant of life parading in front of him each and every day. He's pretty sure in the long run the whole panorama he views is bound to be overrated when it all goes down.

Everyone in the auditorium seems somber and downcast as usual this morning, even if it is Palm Sunday and Jesus was supposed to have entered Jerusalem on his donkey amid shouting and hoopla and joy, but Ray is used to a certain absence of happiness on Sunday mornings. He first noticed it years ago, and he's working on a way to get away from it as soon as possible. He doesn't know if another religion is an option, since he'll probably be disappointed by some other group too, so he thinks the best way to conquer this Sunday morning feeling of despair is to get a job somewhere where his presence would be required on Sundays. There are some stores starting to open on Sundays in Nashville, fighting against the restrictions called Blue Laws, and maybe he can get hired at one of those places. His parents will get ticked as hell about it, but once they get used to the idea that they don't have to shell out any money to him for anything anymore they'll go right back to adoring his brother and sister and allow him to fade from view little by little until he can't be spotted.

He's been allowed to drive the Galaxy to church this morning, since he'd done his best to dawdle and be late so he wouldn't have to go with the rest of the family. Besides, Albert always likes to drive his Fairlane in on Sunday mornings so all the men can see how clean it is and how fine it ran and be overly envious of how he had such a nice car while they were driving used pieces of metal that will never appear in a fancy car magazine or get driven by a celebrity who doesn't have to worry about how much he brings home a week. Ray likes being in a car all by himself so he can leave and drive home whenever and whichever way he wants.

He sees the red Cadillac in his mirror just before he turns on his street, which isn't hard to do since the Cadillac's bright presence is akin to an A-Bomb test with all its light and flashiness. People driving along the highway couldn't have missed it if they tried. Maybe if they were Ray Charles, but then, they probably wouldn't be driving if they were.

Uncle Jack has the top down, and this time Conway Twitty croons out of the speakers and into the thin air of the neighborhood. Ray looks around to see if any of the neighbors are noticing, but for now the yards are empty and no one is in sight, and Ray doesn't know if he is relieved about that fact or not. A part of him is like his mother and dad—he doesn't want anyone to know too much about Uncle Jack, because they are things he does that might be embarrassing. But there is another part of him that is all himself, and in that sub-section he wouldn't mind if everyone looked out their windows or stood on their lawns and remarked to each other about the loud music and the big red Cadillac that must have cost a fortune and the questionable woman that had been in the car that day those few years ago and Jack Patterson himself, who it seems and appears may not be as devout and clean-living as his sister and brother-in-law at all. Ray wouldn't mind it very much whatsoever if Uncle Jack let everyone on occasion see what kind of life he is living that is different than theirs and how the grass may not only be somewhat greener on his side but might even be a totally different color altogether.

"Didn't know if you'd be out of bed by now or not," Jack says as he walks up the porch steps. "Sometimes that particular brand of whiskey you had last night can grab a fellow by the throat and drag him down for a while. It can be rough sledding if a fellow isn't used to it."

Ray ponders for a second whether to tell his uncle the events of the night before with the touchy-feely floozy and her singing companion and the Jameson bottle that met such an untimely death, but he feels like his uncle might be disappointed in him if he finds out there is no romantic tall tale to tell, so he smiles instead and shakes Jack's hand and says no, he's all right, he feels just fine. There, he thinks, at least Uncle Jack won't think I'm an absolute fuckup who can't even hold his liquor before he drinks it.

"I'm not going to stay too long," Jack confides, "because I ain't had that much sleep. Me and some folks were out until breakfast this morning, and I think we're booked into doing the same thing tonight, so I've got to go back to the motel and get a little shut-eye before then."

"I thought you were staying with some friends," Ray says. "That's what Mom said. I didn't know you were staying at a motel where you have to pay. You could have stayed here. There's an empty bed in John's room. He's not coming home until next weekend."

"Now do you honestly think I could stay here with your mother any length of time without there being a big argument and fight getting started?" Jack grinned and shook his head. "Anyway, if I pulled some of my usual tricks your daddy would punch me in the nose in front of his children and the neighbors and God and everybody."

They walk into the living room where the television is on but there's no one watching. On the screen is an old episode of "I Love Lucy." Lucy Ricardo and Ethel Mertz are up to some sort of foolishness, and the audience titters in the background. Pretty soon Ray knows everyone is going to begin to die laughing and then applauding like hell, and he doesn't want to hear it right now. He walks over and switches it off. His mother is off in the kitchen, clattering pans and starting to prepare Sunday dinner. His dad is in the garage already, running a rag across his Fairlane to get rid of whatever dust it has collected on its trip to church this morning. His sister is upstairs talking on the phone and his brother is two hundred miles away doing who knows what on a Sunday in a college town. He is not sure of what that might be. He knows what it would probably be if it was his Uncle Jack or himself in that city with a lot of alcohol and girls walking around loose. John, Ray knows, is doing nothing of the sort. Ray can't wait for when the time comes for him to have his chance. He already knows he won't be anything like John. He'll have some fun wherever it is he'll be.

"How many hours a week have you been working?" Uncle Jack asks.

"As many as I can get," Ray says. "The more I work, the quicker I can buy a car."

"What kind of car have you been thinking about?"

"Well, it isn't going to be a Ford, I can tell you that for sure." Ray looks around the room to see if by chance anyone might be listening. "I'm so tired of Fords I hope I never see one again. I want something different."

"There are a lot of good cars out there."

"I want a Chevy," Ray says decisively. "A Super Sport. I want one with bucket seats and four in the floor with some nice wheels. Maybe a convertible, but I haven't made up my mind about that just yet."

"Have you looked at any?"

"There's one down at the lot I like a lot. It's red like your car. It's got black bucket seats, but it's an automatic in the floor. It's a lot more than I can afford."

"Ain't nothing wrong with an automatic," Jack says. "Mine's an automatic. You don't ever have to worry about burning your clutch out and having to get a new one.

Clutches cost a lot of money. Besides, with an automatic you always have one hand that's free. That hand comes in handy when you've got a little girl sitting up there in the front seat beside you."

"I don't have that to worry about," Ray says. "I have trouble even getting a date sometimes."

"You'll have plenty to worry about," Jack laughs. "You get a car like what you're talking about and girls will be calling you up for dates. Believe me, I know how girls are. They like riding around in something fancy. It makes them real easy to get along with."

Jack studies his wristwatch and looks up at Ray.

"You're out of school all week, right?"

"Yeah, but I have to work every day."

"How much money do you have saved so far?"

"About four hundred dollars," Ray says, ashamed about how pitifully poor he truly is. "That's not anywhere close to buying a car, and Daddy won't let me finance one."

"I'll come down to see you at the lot tomorrow. We'll take a look at this car you're telling me about."

"Okay."

"Now let me go in and say something to your mother and get out of here. I've got to get me some sleep sometime."

~~~~~

Uncle Jack is as good as his word. Ray hasn't been at work two hours Monday when Jack walks in the door of the prep room and holds up a hand in greeting. He stops and lights a Lucky with his shiny Zippo, then walks over to where Ray is waxing a 1965 Mustang, which his boss is fixing to roll out on the lot and make all kinds of money on. It had been bought last week at an auction; probably his boss had come across it because some dumbass had gone out and put a down payment on it and then couldn't keep up the notes. Ray sees cars come through like this all the time, and that's just with him working here part-time. Seeing it so much has made him careful with his car shopping. He'd hate like hell to put all his money into getting a car and then not being able to afford it and having some asshole repossess it and leave him without any money or a car. He'd be worse off that way than he was now—if that is possible.

"I thought you didn't like anything that has a Ford emblem on it," Uncle Jack says.

"I didn't mean Mustangs," Ray says. "They're different. They ain't been around long enough for the Ford Company to ruin them yet. They will though, you watch and see. They'll get cheap and change everything that's good and mess it all up. You know how it is—fix or repair daily." Ray recites this like it's this great witticism, like Uncle Jack probably hasn't heard it yet. It sort of hangs in the air stupidly, though, and Ray regrets saying it. He's pretty sure there's next to nothing Uncle Jack hasn't heard sometime before, so he doesn't know why he's wasting his breath like this. He needs to play it cool.

"Ain't nothing wrong with a Ford that ain't wrong with everything else. They all got their good points and their bad."

Jack peers in the Mustang's window at the backseat behind the driver's side.

"I'll tell you what's wrong with this car right off the bat," he says. "I'd never buy a car that had a backseat as tiny as this one. Maybe this car is made for boys who've got big houses or apartments, or can afford a motel room every time they take a girl out on an evening, but for most of us members of the male population a car with a big backseat comes in pretty handy most of the time. Hell, you couldn't even escort a girl back there and have a decent conversation in this car. You'd be too busy trying to get comfortable to even open your mouth, much less be trying to do anything else."

Ray decides to smile and keep his mouth shut and go on massaging the quarter panel with a cloth, maybe let his uncle decide what else they're going to talk about.

"You got a minute where you can show me this Chevy you've been telling me about?"

Ray leads Jack out the door and straight ahead to where the back row of the car lot is. On this back row are all the clunkers that the kids and the poor people come in and buy. Most of them are ten years old at least, with dents and rust and maybe a windshield with a crack in it, and stenciled on the windows are phrases like "Good Buy!" and "Good Hunting and Fishing Car" and "Runs Good!" Ray is never asked to wax these cars or shine them up or even vacuum them out much. All he has to do is hose them off and get rid of the crushed bugs and birdshit and they're ready to sell. He always looks them over and wonders why anyone would waste their money on them, but all he has to do is go to school for a week and come back on Friday afternoon and most of them are gone already. It makes him realize that's why his boss has them around, because there's a lot of people who can't afford to get anything that's not back here in the last row.

Ray walks Jack up front to the corner of the second row. That's where the 1963 Super Sport is. It's red like the Eldorado and it has black bucket seats and an automatic in the floor. The body is pretty good. It may have been in a wreck at one time but there's no bondo he can see or feel. There aren't any tears in the interior but for a little gash up by the tachometer. You have to really look to see it. The clock doesn't work because the minute hand is missing, but the radio sounds good. Whoever owned it before put two more speakers in the back behind the seats. Ray has looked it over good when it came in. He tried not to make it look too good, since if he did somebody might come along and buy it, and right now he doesn't want that to happen.

Jack walks around the car like a hawk circling. He runs his hand along the white strip across the side panels and moves his hand back and forth on the taillights to see if they're loose. He stops for a moment to peruse the windshield crack, but it must not be important because he makes no comment about it. The tires seem to pass muster too. He doesn't kick them or anything.

"Have you driven it yet?" he asks.

"Not yet. I've started it up and listened to it idle some."

"Go see if it's okay if we take it for a ride."

Ray walks up the trailer steps where Bobby Porter and his wife Mary Ann have their offices. Mary Ann sits at a desk in front with a telephone and a typewriter and a mimeograph machine she can make copies of contracts and advertising ads with. Mary Ann was probably not a bad-looking woman twenty-five years ago, but now she is getting fat and wrinkly and the only one in the world who doesn't know it is her. Bobby sits in the back at a desk with a window so he can see if anybody is in the lot looking at a used car, in which case he can jump up and slip on his madras sport coat and amble outside for a potential sale, always saying to Mary Ann or me or his mechanic Howard the same thing every time, "Looks like we might have a nibble." Sometimes he'll reel a fish in, sometimes not. Ray guesses he does okay. Bobby's been in business for as long as Ray can remember.

"Hey, Mr. Porter, is it okay if my uncle and I take that 63 Chevy around the block?"

"Is that your uncle out there? I was wondering who was driving that Caddy parked out front. I never saw him come in."

"He's been in the back talking to me. He came by to take a look at the Chevy."

"Why would he want the Chevy when he's driving that Eldorado already? Tell him if he wants to trade I'll do it even, but I can't afford to pay out the kind of money that car of his is worth."

"He's just looking at it for me. I told him I liked it."

"I didn't know you wanted that car, Ray. You never said anything about it."

"I haven't got the money for it is why. I just mentioned I liked it and he wanted to take a look."

"Sure, go ahead," Bobby said. He opens up a stick of Spearmint gum and looks at it before he pops it into his mouth. "Just don't peel all the rubber off the tires before you bring it back."

Ray takes the keys off the peg on the wall and walks back toward the car. Uncle Jack is already sitting in the passenger seat.

"You want me to drive?" Ray asks.

"You're the one in love with it," Jack says. "I wouldn't want to break your heart and take away what you've been looking forward to."

"My boss might not like me driving it right now. I may have given him the impression you were interested in it for yourself."

"I already have a car," Jack says. "It's parked right over there." He points with his left hand at the Cadillac, the cigarette burning between his fingers, sending smoke upwards toward the headliner and swirling out the window, sending a message to Ray he hasn't considered until now.

"You're the one needing a car," Jack says. "You're the fellow that needs to know if it runs good enough for him."

"I don't have enough money saved yet."

"Four hundred dollars will pay your insurance," Uncle Jack says. "You just drive it a few minutes and see if you still like it. Let me worry about the rest. I'll have me a little chat with your boss."

~~~~~

42

Uncle Jack talks Bobby Porter down, then peels off eight one hundred dollar bills from his billfold and hands the title over to Ray.

"You keep that money you've saved up," he tells Ray. "Right now I'm going to see about getting you some insurance. I can do better than four hundred dollars."

Ray is not the most talkative person in the world, and he isn't a mute either, but at the moment he doesn't know what to say to his uncle other than thank you. He watches the Cadillac disappear down the highway toward Nashville and tries to imagine himself as the owner of the 1963 Chevrolet Super Sport that is parked in front of him. It is hard to do. Maybe by washing the advertising paint off the windows it might make it clearer in his head. At least it might stop someone from coming in off the street and trying to buy it. He tapes the temporary tag on the back window. He puts the keys in his pocket. He guesses his uncle is gone to get his insurance. By the time he finishes work at one he will be able to drive home in his own car. He won't have to call Jimmy or any of his other friends for a ride. He won't have to walk a mile and a half if he can't find anybody. It is hard to believe how everything has changed. It is hard to believe that he is finally going to get a chance to start living like everybody else has been doing for the longest time while he's stood by and watched.

There is, of course, this nagging little thought in the back corner of his mind. He is trying to imagine what his mother is going to say when he drives the Chevy home today. He is trying to go over what he is going to tell her when she looks out the window and sees what is sitting in the driveway. He thinks further about his dad coming home from work before dinner and what he might say. It isn't a Ford—that is for sure—but somehow Ray doesn't think the make or model of his car truly matters that much. What will matter is how it has ended up being his. What matters is it has come from Uncle Jack. It doesn't matter that Uncle Jack had financed Brenda's birthday pizza party or helped John get the Falcon he's gone to school in; what went on for the benefit of Brenda and John is always going to be fine. But it is different with him, and Ray knows it. There is a different set of rules for him from John and Brenda, all because he has always been the child operating outside the parental orb somewhat, not in a manner that was so bad and revolutionary or anything anyone could put their finger on and mark as true and undisputed evidence of the fact, but still a different code of conduct that he was unspokenly supposed to adhere to that his brother and sister did not. In his mind he knows already it is not going to be just hunky and dorey that Uncle Jack has financed his new car. The Super Sport will sit in the driveway as a symbol to his mother and father of their middle son's sudden and soon to be expanding independence from them.

So it is going to be a little tricky. He'll have to stay on his toes and say all the right things.

He leaves the lot at one and ventures down Main on his first drive as an official car owner. There isn't all that much traffic out, but he is convinced all the other drivers are out to get him anyway. He imagines them running red lights—even if there are only two in town—and crashing into him at four-way stops. In his mind he imagines the city police taking notice of him and pulling him over on some false pretense, giving him a bogus ticket for some violation he had never thought existed. He inches and crawls and finally turns into the Burger Chef, which is about the only place in town young people frequent. There is no one inside when he enters, even though school is out and there are not that many other places for kids to go, but he now has a surplus four hundred dollars at his disposal that he didn't have this morning when he got out of bed, so he figures he can afford a hamburger and french fries and a strawberry milkshake if he wants. If he couldn't treat himself every now and then, why was he even bothering to work?

He takes his time eating. It is probably the longest lasting cheeseburger he's ever consumed, what with dallying over the fries and politely sipping his milkshake. He is in the booth a good half hour when a Dodge Coronet pulls in beside his car and three girls get out. Recognizing Ann Caldwell and Cheryl Thompson and Patsy King, he starts to interrupt this prolonged session and get out the door before he has to undergo the agony of catching the attention of these three girls from his class and being completely ignored by them like always, which is consistently damaging to his ego whenever it occurs, but could at least sometimes be shaken off by not having contact with anybody when there was no doubt you were getting overtly ignored because you weren't worthy enough to garner any attention. Anyway, Ray has put off going home with his new car long enough. He knows he is going to have to face his parents with its presence sometime. It isn't like he can hide it somewhere and pretend it doesn't exist.

He gets up to leave and take the secondary side door out to the other side of the building. Then he can walk around and get in his car without crossing the path of the three girls coming in the front. He takes one fleeting look at them before pushing off. God, they are all so good-looking. He doesn't know who he likes the best. There isn't any sense in wondering about it, though. He is nothing to any of them. That's just the way it is.

He is at his car with his hand on the door about to get in when he realizes he's left his keys inside on the table. Sharp thoughts of admonition flash through his head at this tactical mistake, even though it isn't like having a set of car keys to keep up with is a matter of habit with him just yet. He looks through the window and sees Cheryl Thompson looking at him. She says something and the other two girls' heads turn and look his way. He is caught in their gazes and there isn't anything he can do about it. He can't just do an about-face and take off somewhere for safety. He has to go back in the Burger Chef and get his keys. He can't leave his car sitting here just because he is a chicken-shit who is afraid of three people just because they happen to be girls and just because he knows he wants each and every one of them and knows it is just too bad about that, because he is poor and ugly and dumb as a rock on top of everything else.

He decides the best thing to do is to go in with his head down and scoop up his keys without looking up. Perhaps if he makes the mandatory five or six steps to the table quickly and with no fanfare he can grab the keys and be back out the door without being acknowledged. This being acknowledged shit was a two-headed monster anyway. Whichever way it went—being spoken to or not looked at—it was bad either way. Whatever happened would leave some kind of scar. He'd be laughed at as something trivial or he'd be ignored totally because it wasn't worth the energy to show him any attention. He isn't an athlete. He isn't cute or rich. He is just one of those don't matter boys who was out there, like a cloud or a tree or a mailbox, that didn't make much of a difference in anything whatsoever.

When he gets to the booth his keys aren't there. He looks on the floor to see if they've fallen off the table, then starts to walk up to the counter to ask if they've been turned in. That is when he sees Ann Caldwell holding them up in her hand, jingling them like she is a Salvation Army Santa with a bell. She is smiling, all white teeth and cheekbones and black hair like the dead of night down a road where nobody lives.

"Did you lose something?" She shakes the keys to make the sound one more time. "I was hoping no one would come back after these, because I bet they go to that pretty red car that's parked out there." She turns and looks out the window at the Super Sport. "I was hoping maybe it would be finder's keepers and I'd get to keep it all for myself."

Since this is the first time Ann Caldwell has spoken to him since eighth grade, Ray doesn't know how to respond at first. But there is something about the fact that the keys Ann holds in her fingers belong solely to him now, and those keys undisputedly are a part of the 1963 Super Sport sitting outside, visible as it is to these three heretofore unapproachable females. Ray has the swift and sudden realization in his mind that the rules of the game have suddenly changed for him, just from this very day. With the addition of the Super Sport to his arsenal he has now elevated his status from being a bottom-scraping nobody to a person who is all at once visible on the radar of whatever field this new game is being played upon. All at once he doesn't give a shit what his parents are going to say when he gets home. He will gladly trade the static they're going to give him for the look in Ann Caldwell's eyes and the smile on her face this instant.

"I had some other stuff on my mind," he tells Ann Caldwell. He smiles at her and smiles at her friends, looks them all in the eye to see if they're ready for the new him or not. He decides the three of them all pretty much don't know what to make of him.

"If I was rich and had cars to give away," he tells Ann, "you'd certainly be the first person on my list. But since I'm poor as a church mouse and all my money is invested in that piece of metal out there, I'll have to pass on it this time."

"I didn't really need it," Ann says. "I've got my own car to get me around." She motions outside at the Dodge Coronet. "I just thought your car was cute, that's all."

Ray sees an opening and decides to take it. He tells himself he's chicken if he doesn't.

"You can ride in it any time you want, you know," he says. "All you have to do is tell me when."

Ann smiles at this.

"I'm afraid my boyfriend wouldn't like that too much. You know Tommy Cutler, don't you? We're going steady, and me riding in your car wouldn't do a whole lot to make him happy."

She is smiling as she says this, like she is waiting for him to say something stupid so she can put him back in his place. She hasn't figured out yet that Ray is not going to return to his previous habitat anytime soon, maybe never.

"Well," he says, "you can always change your mind down the road." He takes the keys from her hand and makes sure he touches her as he does it. "You can change your mind about a lot of things, whether it's Tommy Cutler or riding in a car or whatever." He smiles at the three of them one more time. "It's a free country, that's for sure. You can do what you want to."

~~~~~

Wondering exactly what he is going to say when he gets home, Ray is close to overjoyed when he rounds the corner of Montgomery Road and spots Uncle Jack's Cadillac parked out front. It is almost as if his uncle has realized what a delicate situation Ray was going to be coming home to and has decided to come by for a visit and maybe deflect a little of the tension that is bound to appear over Ray and his new addition to the family. Ray just hopes Uncle Jack has been telling Loretta some of his funny stories and making her laugh in spite of herself, since he is the only one in the world capable of making his mother act somewhat human. Ray asks God to make sure his mother is in the best mood possible.

He finds the two of them sitting on the back patio drinking iced tea. It is a nice enough spring day, not altogether warm but certainly not cool and no wind to speak of, so Loretta and Jack sit on a swing with their backs to the sun, and it looks to Ray like his mother is in the throngs of actually enjoying a visit from her brother. Lots of times the two seem almost on the edge of a fight, so this is something good to see.

"Hey," Ray says as he pushes through the back door. He is looking into the sun so he holds his hand over his eyes, like he is a frontier scout scouring the landscape for wild savages.

"What do you say there, buddy?" Jack says.

"Your uncle has been telling me you've got something new to show me," Loretta smiles. "I've been sitting here trying to guess what it is. It isn't a new suit to wear to church Easter Sunday and it isn't a pony, so I suppose I'm all guessed out. I have no idea what it is."

"I got a new car," Ray says, glad to go ahead and get this going at last. "Uncle Jack helped me buy it this morning."

"That was going to be my third guess," Loretta says.

She looks at Ray pleasantly, waiting, he thinks, for him to offer up an explanation as to why he would leave the house on a spring morning and do such a thing without discussing it with her and Albert at least one time. He starts to tell her how he didn't feel like waiting another two years or forever for the time to be right for him to get mobile, but he doesn't do it. He decides to be like his mother and smile pleasantly back and let her take it from there, which he knows is not going to be right now but is going to wait and hang in the air until his dad gets home from work. Screw that, he thinks.

"It's a nice car, Loretta," Jack offers. "We got a real good deal on it."

"You'll like it," Ray says. "Come on and look at it. If you're nice I'll even take you for a ride."

"It depends on whether your father will let you keep it or not," she announces, like the jury is still out on this subject.

"Yeah, that's right," Ray smiles, though what he wants to say is there's not too much she or his dad can do about it right this minute, seeing how it was paid for and insured and had drive-out tags on it all in his name. It wasn't like his dad or his mom or anyone was going to order him to drive it back down to the lot and make Bobby Porter take the car back, because the name of the game in this matter was a deal was a deal, and once a guy signs on the bottom line in this world there isn't a whole lot anybody can do to change it later on. That is just the way it is.

Loretta follows Ray and Jack through the house and out the front door. The first time the Super Sport comes into view she has a hard time keeping the smile off her face. It's certainly a pretty car, she thinks, but that doesn't negate the fact that Ray had no business buying it without her and Albert's permission. It was a lot of money for a boy Ray's age to be involved in, and having him go about it this way was not going to teach him anything about being careful with his money. Then she remembers it is Jack's money that has paid for the car and she shouldn't be worrying so much about Ray being loose with his own money. Maybe that takes him off the hook a little, she decides, because she wonders what she would have done in his shoes if an uncle had insisted on buying her the car of her dreams when she was a teenager. Would she have turned him down? She doesn't know, but it still doesn't excuse Ray entirely for going out on his own and doing such a thing.

But it is a pretty car. She has to admit that. Still, though, Jack shouldn't have done it. It doesn't do anything but make her and Albert look bad. She's afraid Ray doesn't listen to them much already, and now with this car it will be just another step out the door and down the road a piece further than he should be going at this stage of his life. She is going to have to have a talk with Jack. She knows he's alone in the world and maybe gets lonesome for family sometimes, but that doesn't mean he needs to keep trying to find a way to buy himself into his relatives' affections.

Besides, Albert isn't going to like this one bit. He might not say too much, but he isn't going to like it.

"Come on," Ray says. "I'll take you for a ride."

Loretta gets in the front seat and Jack climbs into the back. They are backing out the driveway when Brenda rides up on her bicycle and looks at them wide-eyed.

"Whose car?" she asks.

"Mine," Ray says. "Get in. We're going for a ride."

He drives as carefully as possible, taking great caution not to put his foot on the accelerator too much and throw his passengers' heads and bodies back against their seats. He could do it easily; he could scare the royal shit out of everybody with the way the car can jump and buck and growl when he gives it enough gas. He'd tried it out on Highway 41 on his way home from lunch to see what would happen, and what had happened had made him smile. He was already grinning somewhat from his encounter with Ann Caldwell and her friends anyway, and then he heard the big engine snarl and come to life when he ordered it to with his foot, and he was beaming when he finally made himself slow down after a half mile's run. He told himself not to get a ticket and not to have a wreck and kill himself, but, God, wasn't this great! In his head he knew that whatever got said to him and preached to him from then on wasn't going to matter. This was his car and no one was going to take it away from him. There wasn't a thing anyone could do.

He creeps along and shows his mother the radio. He points out the color of the seats and the carpet. He makes note of the dashboard and all its indicators and instruments. This Chevrolet, he tells his mother, has a lot of things different than a Ford. And in the backseat he hears Brenda ask Uncle Jack if when she gets older if he would buy her a car too?

Jack leaves in the Eldorado to meet some friends for dinner, Loretta goes to the kitchen to turn on the television and begin dinner, and Brenda wanders upstairs to her room. Ray sits on the front porch and waits for Albert to come home. He has parked the car in the middle of the front yard so Albert could get by and so there is no way Albert can miss seeing it, and Ray sits on the porch swing and rocks himself back and forth in tune and time with the voice of Eric Burden, who is up there in his head singing "It's My Life." There isn't a radio anywhere around, it is all in his brain, but Ray doesn't care. He can hear it just fine. He sits and rocks and sings the verses over and over while he waits for his dad to get home. This is going to be good, he thinks.

~~~~~

Jack can't just leave his nephew alone to face his dad about the new car, so he makes his way back to his sister's house after dinner to provide some re-enforcement in case things get a little testy on the part of Albert. Jack has nothing against his brother-in-law really, other than the fact Albert seems to have no sense of humor or adventurous spirit whatsoever, preferring, it seems to Jack, to keep to himself in his garage and stay out of the line of fire with Loretta and go to church and go to work without much fanfare at all other than to have everybody think of him as this big mechanical guru who knows everything there is to know about a Ford automobile. Big shit, Jack thinks. I don't know a goddamned thing about a car, but the one I drive is ten times better than anything Albert Roberts has ever owned. All it took was money. Jack always has money. It beats the hell out of knowledge every time. And it isn't that he doesn't have knowledge either. He can drive most anywhere in the country without looking at a map. That's saying something right there.

Ray and one of his friends are shooting basketball at the goal at the front of the driveway. The ball bounces away from the two toward Jack as he approaches. He catches it and dribbles it twice and launches a set shot from far out. The ball banks off the backboard and goes through the netless hoop.

"Boy, that was lucky," Ray says.

"I used to shoot baskets for money," Jack says. "Won me a lot of money playing games of H-O-R-S-E and Twenty-One and Around the World when I was in the service. I can sure as hell beat you two sissies. On one leg I can beat you."

Albert opens the side door and stands there watching. He looks like he has something to say.

"Come on and get in on this, Albert," Jack smiles. "The more the merrier."

"I used to play in high school," Albert says evenly. "I was my team's leading scorer senior year."

"Doesn't matter," Jack says, picking up the ball and examining it for defects. "I can beat all of you with no trouble at all."

The game of H-O-R-S-E begins and it doesn't take long for everybody to see Jack is right. Jack can and is beating them with no difficulty or sweat, almost like this is a play and he is the writer and the director and has the lead role. Ray is the first to go out, then Jimmy. The two boys lean against the porch and watch Albert and Jack play the game out. Albert has four letters and Jack only one, and Ray suspects Jack has missed the one shot he did just to provide Albert a little hope and make the game interesting.

Albert hits four shots in a row, but Jack makes every one behind him, smiling all the time until Albert misses a free throw. Jack looks at his watch as if he has an appointment, then walks nonchalantly to the corner by the trash cans and sinks a twenty footer.

"I have to go," he explains to Albert. "I've got a hot date waiting on me downtown."

Albert, of course, misses. Jack picks up the ball and twirls it on his index finger like he belongs on the Globetrotters.

"Don't feel bad, Albert. You got caught playing my game. I wouldn't dare try to tune up a car against you."

"You sure did put a lot of money into Ray's car this morning," Albert says, changing the subject. "You ought to let me pay you back a little of it."

"Don't worry about it," Jack says. "I haven't got anything better to do with my money than spend it on women and booze and big red Cadillacs. I might as well make somebody in my family happy for a change."

"I'm hoping this boy doesn't get too happy with it. I don't know if he's grown up enough to handle it just yet."

"He may surprise you. He may not be as down to earth as John, but he's not out there in orbit either. He's better than I was when I was his age."

Albert doesn't say anything to that. He wipes his hands on his pants and starts back in the house. "I want to talk to you before you go anywhere in that car," he says to Ray, then goes in the house.

Jimmy is smiling but keeping his mouth shut. Ray looks at the door and then at his uncle.

"At least he hasn't had a stroke about it yet," he says.

"He's close," says Jack. "He's very close. You better try and not give him a reason to have one. The least little thing might send him over the edge."

~~~~~

Ray's idea on Thursday afternoon is to drive to Nashville where Uncle Jack has his motel room a mile from downtown and get something else to drink, but once that

54

task was done he would drive the Super Sport back and park it before the rest of the evening festivities began. Ray still has a yearning to taste some more of that Jameson Irish Whiskey that had been shattered on the ground before he had the chance to acclimate his throat to its taste and enjoy the effects he'd had only a notion of last night, but he isn't dumb enough to consider undergoing this new experience behind the wheel of the car of his dreams. However wonderful drinking Irish whiskey and getting hammered beyond recognition of his name and mind might be, he still isn't going to wrap his new car around a tree for the sake of one evening of bliss. He can have this experience with both feet planted on the ground and maybe not end up being the figure of complete remorse for losing his greatest possession when the sun comes up tomorrow morning. If nothing else in his young life, Ray has learned how to be careful. He knows how to cover his tracks.

There is a part of him that wants to leave the car at home and make Jimmy drive his mother's car into Nashville to find Uncle Jack, but this was his own idea about procuring more whiskey and it was his uncle he was going to use to get it for him, so it doesn't seem right to come up with such a master plan and not be the one spearheading the effort. Plus, there is also the fact that Jimmy has yet to ride in his new car, so Ray knows it is only protocol that he picks Jimmy up and lets him admire it on the twenty mile journey into Nashville. Ray knows Jimmy will pop his eyes out when he gets inside and sees the interior and the dash and hears songs on the four speakers. Ray likes this new feeling of having at last something to show off and be proud of, and he knows it is going to be a while before the feeling goes away. He thinks back to the lunch encounter with Ann Caldwell and her pals. He really liked those girls taking a good long look at his car.

"You're a lucky asshole, you know that?" Jimmy sticks a Marlboro in his mouth and punches the lighter in on the dash and waits. Ray isn't sure if the lighter works or not, so he waits to see what happens. It makes him feel good when the lighter warms and pops out like it is supposed to do.

"I wish to hell I had an uncle like good old Uncle Jack," Jimmy says. He rolls his window down and leans his right arm out the window. He takes a draw on his cigarette and flips his ashes out the window.

"Use the ash tray, dipshit," Ray says. "You flip your ashes like that and all they'll do is blow back in the window and end up in the back seat."

"Excuse me," Jimmy says. "I forgot how you have to keep it so clean and nice there, since it won't be long until you're screwing every girl in Goodlettsville right there in the back seat. I'd hate for one of your new love interests to get their clothes soiled or anything."

The Beatles are on the radio. "Ticket to Ride." Ray thinks it isn't a bad song at all. The wind blows in the window against his face and the guitars come through the speakers and he feels like punching the gas a little and speeding. He watches the speedometer inch up some, then he lets off the accelerator. He is going to have to watch it. He is going to have to think about it all the time. It is going to be hard to go slow and to not do what he wants to do every time he gets behind the wheel. He could get in trouble real quick if he doesn't take it easy.

He sees Uncle Jack's Cadillac in the courtyard outside the long motel building, its red fins sticking out like a beacon in a neighborhood of gray drab poverty. The spring day, being somewhat warm for the week before Easter, has risen enough for Jack to have his unit door open to cool things off some. As he gets closer Ray can see his uncle sitting in a fold-up chair by the door outside, reading a newspaper with a glass in his hand. Jack has on an undershirt and Ray can see his belly pooching out and the sun glancing off his thinning hair. Jack doesn't look quite so young this afternoon.

"You look like you're taking it easy," Ray says.

"I'm getting over last night is what I'm doing," Jack grins, although it appears to hurt him to make such a gesture. "This is what they call hair of the dog that bit me," he says, nodding at the drink in his hand. "Old Charter. Another one of those potions you might consider avoiding if you have anything pressing to do over the next week."

"I've never had that either," Ray says.

"How'd you like that Jameson's the other night?"

Ray considers lying and acting like he'd been able to handle it fine, but Jimmy begins laughing in his hyena way, so Ray figures he might as well tell the truth about it.

"I liked it just fine, what little I had. The bad part of it was I found out the bottle wasn't unbreakable."

Ray tells the story of the man and the floozy downtown and how the Irish whiskey had ended up soaking into the sidewalk. Jack laughs and sets his paper down and lights a cigarette. The click of his Zippo when he closes the cover makes a sharp abrupt sound, like it is commenting on how life could be just so unfair sometimes.

"It might as well have gotten broke," Jack says, "because it sounds to me like that woman was trying to take it away from you anyway. Maybe since it got broken she didn't have any hard feelings about it. I know some women who'd kill you for a bottle once they get going. After a stretch some women don't act like ladies at all if there's a bottle of booze involved."

"A bottle of booze is sort of the reason we're here," Ray smiles. "We were wondering if maybe you could get us another bottle of something this afternoon. I wouldn't be asking so soon again, but we're on spring break and we wanted to do something fun. We didn't get much of a chance to the other night."

"I want you to be careful," Jack says. "I don't want you two to go riding around in your new car and have something bad happen."

"No, we aren't going to do anything like that," Ray reassures him. "We're going to be on foot. We'll probably hike over and sit around on the cliffs above the road into town."

"What do you want? Jameson's, like the other night?"

"That would be all right. Whatever you think we might like."

"I should have brought some moonshine down and let you try that out. Some white lightning. You'd have some fun with that for sure." Jack stands up and walks inside the door, stepping back out with a shirt and his billfold. "There's a store across the street about a block up. You boys wait here and I'll be back."

He walks up the road with his hands in his pockets, like he is taking a stroll in the park. Ray looks at the drink his uncle has left by the chair. There are a couple of fingers of brown liquid with an ice cube meandering at the top. He lifts the glass up and smiles at Jimmy.

"To your health," he says, and takes a long gulp. It is strong stuff and he wants to gag and spit it out, but he keeps it down, even though two tears fall from his eyes and rest on his eyelids. "God," he tells Jimmy.

"You better watch it," says Jimmy. "You'll throw up all over his front porch."

Five minutes pass and Jack crosses the street in front of them. He is carrying a brown paper bag in his hand and has a fresh cigarette stuck in his mouth. Ray wonders if maybe he should take up smoking. Maybe a cigarette helps you keep the alcohol down better.

"I decided you don't need Jameson's," Jack says, handing the bag to Ray. "That stuff just makes you crazier than a two-dick dog, and it seems to me you boys are crazy enough already. This here is some Tennessee sipping whiskey from down Lynchburg way, like I told you about. This is Jack Daniel's. It doesn't get any better than this. But once again, you have to promise me you'll be careful."

"We will," Ray tells him.

The bottle gets stashed under the driver's seat, even though Jimmy wants to break the seal and try a taste of it on the way back. No, Ray tells him, strong in his resolve, that's for tonight. We're not about to start drinking it right now in the middle of the afternoon.

Maybe they will go shoot some basketball this afternoon down at the community center or maybe they will see what is going on down in the square, but on a whim Ray drives toward the Burger Chef to see if there is anything happening there, and he sees the car parked there that he'd seen yesterday when he'd stopped for lunch, so he pulls in to see if Ann Caldwell is inside with her friends again.

She is. She is sitting with Sharon Tidwell at a booth in the back, and Ray isn't surprised at all when she waves at him when he walks in. It would have been noteworthy or even a miracle for him and Jimmy to get waved at by two of the best-looking girls at school if it had occurred anytime before yesterday, but Ray somehow knows that things are different now than they were before, that now, with the addition of his red 1963 Chevrolet Super Sport with the bucket seats and the mag wheels the playing field has instantly become a lot more level. As a matter of fact with the way he has seen Ann look at the car the day before he is pretty sure the field has tipped in his favor. He isn't the least bit afraid of being turned down if he asks her to go somewhere with him, which he does after he orders a vanilla malt and sits down in the booth beside her. Not only does he get Ann to go out with him without letting her boyfriend know, but he manages to get Sharon to say yes to go out with Jimmy too. They will double-date. They will go out to a drive-in movie. There is a double feature at the Star

View tonight, Godzilla Meets King Kong or something like that. It doesn't matter what is on, though—Ray knows that. He just keeps thinking about the bottle beneath his seat and how it is more than enough to get them all drunk. He tells himself he is allowed to forget about being out in his car with a bottle of whiskey and how he'd vowed he wasn't going to do anything stupid like that.

That was before Ann Caldwell was involved. At this stage of the Easter break a girl like her is worth taking a chance for.

The arrangements are made to pick the girls up at seven. It will be getting dark by then, and by the time they get to the Star View the movies will be ready to start. Ray already has it in his head how he will use the first feature to add whiskey to Ann's drink—and Sharon's too if she wanted some—and hopefully, by the time the second movie is set to begin, Ann Caldwell will be drunk and maybe he can get a little further along with her than he's ever dared to dream about. He's heard of such things being done by guys ahead of him before, and it seems like a gift from God that right this night he is finally going to be doing it too. Such luck with a girl has never happened to him before, and he is so excited when he gets home he has trouble going through the routine of cleaning up and dressing.

He doesn't want to go to the trouble of walking to the concession stand time after time for drinks and ice, so he decides to stop at the grocery store to get some Seven-Up and Coke and ice so he won't have to hike back and forth the whole night. He plans on being busy doing something else during that time.

It is a funny feeling when he comes back out to his car, because where he walks to with his ice and his Seven-Up and Coke there isn't anything there for him to set his stuff in and get in and drive away in. He looks around the small Bi-Rite parking lot and there are only nine or ten cars parked there, and he imagines a few of them belong to the people who work inside. There are three Chevrolets, but none of them are Super Sports. They are Biscaynes and Bel-Airs and Dodges and Plymouths and Fords, but none of them are his car. It is like it is someone's idea of a joke or something, and he looks around to see if someone is hiding and about to burst out laughing at his bewilderment and the way he is turning in circles trying to locate something that just isn't there.

It takes him a few moments before it dawns on him that no one is hiding and laughing and that his car is not present because somebody has taken it. He feels around in his pockets and realizes that while being immersed in his deep thoughts about the coming evening he has gone into the Bi-Rite and left his keys in the ignition of the car. Since he has never owned a car before and never has had to worry about leaving his keys in one, and because he has never had an unopened bottle of Jack Daniel's whiskey before either with the expectation of having a girl swallow its contents down and perhaps allowing him to do things with her body he has never been fortunate enough to experience, he realizes now he has not been thinking very practically and responsibly. He mainly realizes he has not been thinking much at all.

It is not his favorite moment of Easter Break. He is going to have to go inside and ask to use their phone. He is going to have to call his dad. He needs to call the police. He will have to call Jimmy and tell him what happened, and he will have to call Ann and tell her the date is off. He dreads talking to anyone, but he dreads having to break the news to Ann the most. He wonders if his car is gone forever if that meant she was gone from him too? He also wonders about what might happen if and when the Super Sport gets found and the bottle of whiskey gets discovered under the seat. Would he get arrested for possessing alcohol as a minor? Could he convince everyone that the thief had left it behind? He wishes he could call Uncle Jack and see if he could help him. His uncle would know what to do in a situation like this.

Ray has a lot of things on his mind. None of them are all that wonderful.

~~~~~

Even though it classifies as an emergency, Ray is still not too happy to see Albert arrive on the scene first. He would have preferred Uncle Jack showing up or Jimmy in his mother's car or even the police, although Ray knows he wouldn't have had the first idea of what to say and what to not say. But he would have still liked to face their barrage of questions and intimidating legal presence better than having to begin to answer the first wave of questions from his father, who might possibly turn Ray's status as a victim into a verdict of guilt by the time all was said and done.

"You didn't leave the keys in the ignition?" Albert asks right off the bat, like he's certain this is exactly the kind of thing an irresponsible boy like Ray would do. Despite the fact it is true, Ray still resents the question. He knows his dad would never ask John this kind of a question in a circumstance such as this. Of course, John would never be in a circumstance like this to begin with, but that is beside the point.

Ray starts to say he dropped them in the store and someone ran over and snatched them up and took off with the car, but he knows where that sort of response is going to lead to already, so he decides he might as well tell the truth and let Albert go ahead and blow sky high and get it over with. It's going to happen anyway, so it might as well be now. He only wishes his mother were here too, so she could join in and they could have a hemorrhage in stereo.

"Yeah," he says, "I left them in the ignition."

"What did you do something as crazy as that for?" Albert asks.

Ray is about to answer and say how he just woke up this morning and decided a fun thing to do would be to let somebody steal his new car and how he thought he could make it easier for that to happen by leaving the keys in the car so the thief wouldn't have to go through all the trouble of hotwiring it; but before he can say anything, a police car with two cops inside pulls up and sits with the motor running, so Ray takes this to mean he should escape his father's third degree and go over to the policemen and tell them what happened with a few little choice details omitted from the narrative.

He stands beside the cruiser for about a minute before the cop inside rolls his window down and looks at him. Ray can already tell nobody's in too much of a hurry to get the facts and start out in pursuit of his stolen car. He wants to be a smart ass and tell them to take their time and try to relax, but he knows this would accomplish about as much as smarting off to his dad, so he decides to stand there and wait like he has all the time in the world and a thing like a stolen car is just one of those things that happens to him every day.

"You the one who's had his car stolen?" the cop behind the wheel asks.

"Yes sir."

"What kind of car was it?"

"It's a 1963 Chevrolet Super Sport." Ray tries to describe the car as if it was a present tense sort of automobile and not a thing of the past. Hearing it described in past tense might be depressing, like it was wrecked or gone forever already and there is nothing that can be done about it. "It's red, a two-door hardtop. It's got a black interior. Bucket seats," he adds.

"Was it stolen from this lot right here?"

"Yes sir. I went in the store to get a couple of things."

"Were the keys in it?"

Ray wants to scream out yes. He wants to fall on his knees and admit what a stupid dumbass he is to these two cops and his father and anybody else around who might want to hear. There's already a few onlookers watching and trying to figure out what's going on, so maybe they'd be interested in hearing him confess his shortcomings too. Why keep it a secret? Why not just announce it to the whole world? He would for damn sure hate for anybody to get left out.

Jimmy and Uncle Jack pull in at about the same time. When the Cadillac parks beside the police cruiser it serves to pull the attention away from Ray and what an idiot he is and over to the shiny red conglomeration of metal and iron that has just appeared. It appears to Ray that no one in the vicinity has ever seen such a vehicle as the Eldorado before, and this also seems to include the two police officers. They get out of their patrol car and walk by the Cadillac and take a good once-over of the interior, the big dashboard with all its instrumentation and the immense steering wheel, the big white-wall tires, the fins. Jack gets out of the car with his sunglasses on and stops long enough to light a cigarette before walking around the cruiser and up to Ray and Albert.

"Damn, son," he says to Ray, "if you didn't like the car we could have gone back and traded it for another one. You didn't have to just give it away to the first guy who came along."

"I left the keys in it while I went inside," Ray explains. "Somebody took off in it."

"I wouldn't worry about it too much," Jack said. "It isn't like they spent a long time planning to steal it. They'll probably just take it for a little ride and then leave it somewhere. I see it happen all the time up in Clarksville. Them soldier boys get a few drinks in them and they just take off in the first car they see. They run the gas out of it or get to where they want to go and that's it. Heck, I've even been known to filch somebody's wheels myself, just so I could get to where I needed to be. Sometimes I'd even bring it back after I was through." He grins at Albert and pokes him in the belly. "The trick was always getting out of the car and being gone before the cops had the chance to catch you in it."

Albert doesn't speak, but instead walks over to where the two policemen are filling out a report when they take time away from looking at Jack's Cadillac. Ray looks at Jimmy and shrugs his shoulders, which is an unspoken way of saying the evening is shot already. Jack studies his cigarette, which he's got the best of by now, and flicks it away to watch where it lands. He doesn't say anything for a minute, like he's lost in thought about something.

"They still got that drag strip up on the ridge?" he asks, like there's a light bulb turned on in his head all of a sudden.

"You mean Union Hill?" Ray says. "Yeah, it's still there. People go up there on Saturday nights to watch the races. There's all kinds of cars they race on Saturday nights."

"What happens up there during the week?"

"I don't know," Ray says. "Nothing, I guess."

Jack walks over to where Albert and the policemen are standing and says something to Albert. He turns around and motions to Ray to come get in the Cadillac.

"We're going to take a ride," Jack tells him.

Jack doesn't say anything for a minute or two as he drives north and makes a left on Clarksville Highway. The air gets a little cooler the further down the highway they travel, and when Jack turns off on a side road the speed signs and markers all disappear and it appears to Ray that the Eldorado is headed for oblivion. He doesn't want to be a baby about it, but he wishes his uncle would put the top up on the car, because there's a pretty good breeze rushing through the back seat now. He also wishes Jack would turn off WSM or whatever he's listening to, all that Ernest Tubb and Loretta Lynn stuff, and put on something that plays some rock and roll or just turn it off completely. Well, maybe not completely turned off. If it gets too quiet he is afraid he'll have to answer some more of his dad's questions. At least the noise of the radio is keeping his dad silent, which is a good thing right now.

"I ought to be a private eye," Jack mutters. He turns Tammy Wynette off just when she and George Jones begin a duet and steps on the accelerator. "Look up there," he says.

Ray sits up in the back and looks through the front windshield down the narrow road ahead. About a football field away he sees the back lights of his Super Sport moving along at a fast clip. He almost wants to tell Uncle Jack to slow down so whoever is driving the Super Sport won't keep going faster trying to get away and lose control of the car. He keeps his mouth shut, though, because he knows Uncle Jack isn't going to slow down a bit now no matter what.

"Hold on tight," Jack says.

Ray looks at his father in the middle of all this and sees his dad bracing himself against the dashboard with his left hand and holding on to the window panel with his right. The muscles in his jaw are taut and his eyes are almost shut, in one sense like he doesn't want to see what is fixing to happen and in the other he does so he can be prepared for whatever horrible thing is surely on the way. The speedometer sits on sixty, which is to Ray about twice as fast as they need to be going, and the big engine beneath the Cadillac's hood is making a deep-throated roaring sound like a jungle animal having the time of its life. Ray knows his Super Sport is fast and all that, but he can visibly tell the Cadillac is gaining on it. It is not a matter of cars and engines and power, he realizes, but it is because his uncle is one hell of a driver. He watches his uncle with both of his hands on the wheel and his eyes fixed on the winding road ahead, and Ray can almost detect the trace of a smile on Jack's face. He imagines Jack's eyes alight beneath the sunglasses he is wearing, and it comes to Ray that his uncle is enjoying himself. It appears to Ray that Jack Patterson is having the time of his life.

When the Eldorado swings around a curve the Super Sport sits ahead at the side of the road with the passenger door open. Down the hill toward what is probably somebody's farm two figures are running for all they are worth, and try as he may, Ray can't see them clearly enough to know whether he recognizes them or not. He wonders if this chase is going to keep going on foot now. God, he hopes not.

"Let them go," Jack says. He stops his car and shifts it into Park, lights a cigarette and laughs. "They're going to have a hell of a long walk back," he says. He looks over at Albert and pats him on the shoulder. "Hope you didn't crap all over my seat during all this excitement," he smiles. "If you did it's you that's going to have to clean it up."

Ray taps his father on the shoulder so he'll move forward and Ray can get out. He walks over to the Super Sport and peers inside, not seeing anything too much unchanged from two hours ago. He wants to lean down and see if the bottle is still under the seat but tells himself to wait until later. No need to tempt fate, he thinks. Best to be careful for a while.

"Everything looks okay," he calls back. Albert and Jack are still in the Cadillac. Ray can see Jack grinning like he always does. He can't make out what his dad is doing. It's probably not anything he wants to see.

~~~~~

The bottle is still there.

Ray has to wait for the police to come out and finish their report and for his dad to leave and go back home before he can fish under the seat and see if he's been merely joy-ridden or thoroughly burglarized. He has this moment of relief mingled with guilt when his fingers touch the paper bag and feel the alcoholic presence still residing beneath the seat; he feels joyous that he still possesses the means to help rid Ann Caldwell of her precautions once he has her in the proper setting, but he also suffers waves of persistent guilt and foreboding by knowing he has been delivered from a terrible situation with his dad and the police simply by the grace of God, and he'd better repent and be grateful and not traipse headlong down the path he is lately traveling or else things might not go so smoothly this next time and his coming up smelling like a rose at present could shortly turn into a huge shit-pie with his name on it heading squarely for a direct hit on his skull.

Perhaps, Ray thinks, a compromise is in order. Perhaps this Wednesday before Easter is not a good time to push his luck. Thou shalt not tempt the Lord thy God, his inner ringmaster tells him. Better back off a little from this full-scale assault on the Commandments for a day or two at least. Besides, most of the decision has already been made for him. He's called Ann and told her about his stolen car and how he couldn't pick her up this night. To call her back now would make him look like an idiot, like maybe his Super Sport hasn't been stolen at all this day, but maybe Ray is just such a fool that he had gone and parked it somewhere and then forgotten where he'd left it. No, probably this is an omen and he should proceed with care for a while. Maybe he should let Ann stay home and park the car and let Planet Earth take a spin or two before he jumps headlong into the fire again.

But he still has the bottle of Jack Daniels, and he still has the means in Uncle Jack to get more where this bottle came from. So it doesn't seem like too much of a risk on this night for him to take the bottle and share it with Jimmy in a safe environment where there is no Ann

Caldwell or Super Sport present. He deduces a good night's entertainment might be gleaned by Jimmy and him taking the bottle and a couple of cold drinks from the Burger Chef and a transistor radio and climbing the hill behind the Lutheran church and the motel down from City Hall on the other side of the highway toward downtown Nashville and sitting and talking and listening and polishing off the whiskey and having a good time altogether with nothing to worry about other than being able to walk back home later or not.

Yes, Ray decides, that seems like the right thing to do.

Jimmy, who had believed that on this night he would be in the back seat of Ray's Chevy with a girl who previously had never paid attention to him before, isn't nearly so enthralled about Ray's plan for the evening. For one thing, there is the half-mile hike down Dickerson Pike. Then there is the climb up the steep hill behind the motel and the church to where the woods and thickets are. Jimmy isn't crazy about this much effort just so he can hang around for the night with Ray, and for a little bit he would stay at home and watch television with his little brother, but there is the matter of the bottle involved. Jimmy knows how Ray is. If he leaves him alone with the bottle too long there won't be anything left for him. And Jimmy is of the conviction that it is high time he found out about Jack Daniel's and Jameson's Irish whiskey and various other things alcoholic and it might as well be tonight when he starts learning.

It is already dark when they start to climb the hill. Ray explains it is best for the two to be under an inky cloak so no one passing by on the road or visiting at the motel or worshipping at the church might see them and think they might be up to something not so lawful and report them to the authorities. Ray insists on carrying the whiskey because Jimmy isn't the most graceful guy in town, even though

Jimmy has to remind him back that it hadn't been him who dropped the original bottle in the first place.

"That couldn't be helped," Ray says. 'That crazy old bitch knocked it out of my hand."

"Still," Jimmy says.

They stop at a point maybe fifty yards above the Lutheran church, but since it is Easter week, Ray thinks that perhaps the Lutherans have called off Wednesday services like the Baptists and the Church of Christs had so that the congregations could maybe get a little rest and not get burned out before the big events of Holy Week transpire. After all, Maundy Thursday and Good Friday and Easter Sunday were a lot of stuff to deal with and still loom on the horizon, especially when people have jobs to go to and dinners to cook for big family gatherings. And don't forget those Easter egg hunts and filling all those baskets with chocolate bunnies and candy too. Easter, Ray thinks, is getting almost as bad as Christmas. When he was a kid, he'd really liked them both. But he is older now. He is changing. He is starting to realize they are both full of shit. He is starting to think that way about a lot of things.

He uncaps the bottle and sniffs at its contents. A strong alcohol smell rushes through his nostrils, a burning almost tear-inducing sensation that makes him wonder if he is going to be man enough to force this sort of foreign potion down his throat. He doesn't question the thought any further, because he knows he will have to swallow it down no matter what. Jimmy is with him, and if Jimmy does it he will too. And he will also have to get it down his throat and into his body because of the fact that the bottle is here in his hand and in his possession and not being held as evidence by the Goodlettsville Police Department or confiscated by his father as something evil no son of his is ever going to touch. No, whatever fates there are in this world have willed his Uncle Jack to him this week to buy a car and booze just for him so he could finally at long last get his life rolling and blooming and in full-swing, and Ray knows it is now his part and duty to step forth and learn what exiting boyhood is truly all about.

So there is no question about it. It is an order from on high. He is going to drink tonight, he is going to get drunk for the first time in his life, and he is going to see what it is like and what it is all about. He is going to see if he likes this part of being a man.

He already has the sneaky suspicion he will. He is starting to feel like Uncle Jack. He is beginning to become convinced he is crazy too.

He takes the lid off his cola and pours what he thinks is a good mix of whiskey into the cup. Jimmy watches what he does and repeats the process for himself, maybe being a little less liberal in adding the contents that Ray has. They raise their cups toward each other in a sort of farewell toast and drink of the cup tentatively, like they are partaking of some strange communion in some alien religious service they have not worshipped at before. After the first sip Ray does not stop like Jimmy does, but instead raises the cup upward at a better angle so he can swallow as much of the elixir as he can stand. In his mind he likens this process to that of getting a shot at the doctor's or going swimming in water that you already know is going to be bone-chilling cold. What you have to do, he tells himself, is just tell that nurse to stick you and get it over with. Tell yourself there won't be any of this dangling your toe in the water to see if you can stand it or not, but just taking a step back and then running up and jumping in and letting it envelope you all at once, and then you have a big stick in your arm or a big shiver run through all your body and then it is over and done and you are stuck and wet and all that worrying stuff is all in the past. So that is what this drinking was going to be like. He is going to do it fast and quick and not be a baby about it, and then it is going to be over and done and he is going to be able to say he has done it. He has taken another step away from this thing called being a boy and he is traveling on a different road now and up ahead somewhere is the hotel where he can check in as a man.

It isn't the greatest taste in his mouth and his throat protests a little as it is going down, but he likes the furnace-like blast in his stomach when the whiskey arrives down there, like one of those trains pulling a big load of cars that rumble through town sometimes and you have to sit and watch and wait for them to get by because they are larger and more powerful than you and have the right of way until they are completely gone, just like this whiskey traveling to its station and bringing the load it has carried with it. He can feel the cargo being unloaded within him, and he knows now that it is delivered he will have to take it and not send it back. It is a done deal and it is all his now.

It is that moment Ray has been wondering about, but it is past now and he knows he is going to be able to live with it, to do it, and he doesn't have to worry about it anymore. He can tell it wasn't so easy with Jimmy like it has been with him. Jimmy holds his cup in front of his face, looking at it with this pained sad expression, and Ray knows Jimmy doesn't like it much. He wants to tell Jimmy how he isn't supposed to like the taste, he isn't supposed to swallow it down to quench his thirst or reward his taste buds or any of that stuff that is classified as pleasure, but it isn't the kind of thing a guy who is already there can tell another guy who is standing at the portal and unsure whether he can cross over or not. It is one of those things that a guy has to decide for himself. So Ray takes another drink and feels the fire and waits.

"God, this stuff is rougher than a cob," Jimmy says. His voice is pinched and tight, like somebody has wrapped some pliers around his throat and is keeping his larynx from acting right. "Maybe I need to mix it with something else. What I've got going here tastes like shit."

"Try drinking it straight."

"No. I don't think so. I can hardly stand the smell of the stuff by itself."

Ray watches as Jimmy keeps raising the cup up to his lips and then lets it slide back down to his side without a sip. They sit on a bank looking down at the highway, the cars passing with their headlights on seemingly another world away. The whiskey is going down smoother now. He is ready to mix another drink but decides against adding anything. He will just drink it straight with ice.

In an hour or so the night is rushing around him and the world below is even further away than before. Jimmy stands slumped by a tree twenty feet away throwing his guts up into the new spring grass. Ray smells the sickness mixed with wild onions and gets up to move down to where the smell and the sound of sickness is not upon him, because it is not what he wants from this night now. What he wants is somewhere to go where he can be his new self, some kind of music permeating his brain, some form of welcoming ritual that will usher him into this new world he has found this night. He thinks of his car at home and he wants to drive it, but he knows why he is instead high on this hill away from it and Ann Caldwell and all those things that he has known this afternoon as a boy. He will see them again soon enough, the Super Sport and Ann Caldwell and all the rest of these things he has found this week. He will see his uncle and find out a few more things too.

That can come tomorrow. This is tonight.

~~~~~

On Maundy Thursday morning Ray wakes up with a headache he feels can only be lessened by his own personal beheading. Since he can't justifiably chop his own head off he gets out of bed and takes a long soothing shower to purge himself of last night's climbing grime and dirt and wild racing thoughts and having to help Jimmy descend the mountain in a sickened throwing up sort of state, washing everything away so he can show up at the lot and bring a few cars to such a physical shining state that someone with a little extra cash might want to buy one. Whether that happens or not is a moot point. All Ray knows is he needs to go in and work a full day so he'll have money for his date this evening.

He remembers calling Ann when he got home last night, even though it was late and he was drunk for the first time in his life and he should have been worrying more about waking up his parents and having them see the state he was in. But he'd thrown away any caution he had and dialed her number anyway, because he knew she'd be up and she'd told him to call her later and that part of him that was not like who he had been until recently and was suddenly supremely confident and knew she'd be waiting and would answer and he wouldn't have to worry about that part of it at all told him to. He was right, of course, right like he always seemed to be these last few days in this charmed life where he didn't have to pay the price of having a car stolen and illegal liquor was available and hangovers could be shaken off and forgotten just like that. He was growing to like himself on this Easter break and that was different. He'd spent a long time not being his own best pal for quite a while, up until this week had arrived and his ship had finally come in.

He has no idea how he is doing it because he's had no practice in any such thing before, but he seemed to be able to say the right words and be funny and clever and all those things he never thought he'd be capable of doing, and by the time he hung up the phone there was a part of him—and maybe it was the whiskey talking, he told himself, he wasn't truly that naïve about things like this—that believed he had Ann Caldwell already wrapped around his finger and he was going to be able to do anything with her he wanted on Thursday night. He wasn't sure how he'd arrived at such a sure conclusion but he knew it was true anyway, just as sure as he knew he wasn't the same guy he was last week and because of what he was learning from Uncle Jack and because of the Super Sport parked outside he was a changed man forever. Not a boy, he reminded himself, but a man. This was quite a transformation he was going through. He told himself to mark it down and remember it forever.

The work day goes by easily enough. He washed and waxed a Coronet and walked through the lot hosing off the inventory until it was time to go. He can't pick Ann up too early this evening, since she has to go to Maundy Thursday services at First Goodlettsville Methodist and he has to show up for the same ritual at his church. It isn't too long a service though, and he doesn't mind going that much. All the service consists of is people reading passages about Jesus getting betrayed by Judas and getting carted off and how it is so awful and terrible that no one is supposed to talk when the program is over but just walk in silence to their car and leave. Ray abided by the inconvenience of the worship experience as best he could, making certain Albert and Loretta know he is there in attendance, but it still irked him some having to sit through the presentation when his mind is on what he is willing to bet he'll be doing a little bit later. He wants to get up from his pew and get in his car and go and find Uncle Jack. He needs more whiskey for the night, and then he has to pick up Ann and get the festivities underway. He hasn't been to her house before, and he hopes he won't have to make the acquaintance of her parents.

He doesn't. His charmed life continues. He doesn't have to find Uncle Jack to get more alcohol either, but on a hunch stops at a liquor store in north Nashville and pays a guy two dollars to go in and buy a bottle of Jack Daniel's for him. He worries the whole time the man is inside that he might find a side door and take off with the money, but his luck holds and the man appears grinning with a set of teeth where more are missing than are present, and Ray drives away smiling and wondering how long this lucky streak he is on is going to last. He also doesn't have to worry about Jimmy this evening, because Ann's friend Sharon has another date with someone else, so the double-date aspect is off for this night. This is fine with Ray, since he doesn't think he could endure another night of Jimmy gagging and complaining and forcing himself to drink from whatever bottle they had and then possibly getting sick and having that to contend with too. He will be more than fine on his own. Besides, his confidence is such that he doesn't need the presence of others holding him back. All he wants is the opportunity to get Ann Caldwell alone. He doesn't know how he knows it but he still is certain that later on when the time comes he will know exactly what to do. He is surprised he is so cool and calm.

Ann's parents aren't at home when he arrives—out to eat with some of their friends after the Maundy Thursday service, he is told. Ann wears a dark blue dress with a pale blue blouse and a thin yellow sweater to make sure she doesn't get cold in the spring night air. It has been warm all day but is cooling off quickly when they leave Ann's house. It is eight o'clock and the sun is down. In a few minutes it will be entirely dark. There are streetlights to illuminate the way in most of the neighborhoods, but not so many that dark places can't be found if a fellow is ingenious enough to look for them.

The first place they go is to the Burger Chef. Ray goes inside and gets two drinks with a lot of ice to go. While his drinks are being poured he looks out the window at the Super Sport and sees Ann's figure dimly in the passenger seat under the parking lot lights. For a moment a slight shiver travels down his spine and he feels something in his mind tremble, and he doesn't know what to make of such a sensation. Is he frightened of this next step he is taking in leaving his boyhood behind? Or is this feeling a warning and a portent of something not so good to come? Even at age seventeen he has always considered himself to be far above average when it comes to sensing something or having a perception about what is down the road hidden from view, and he doesn't know whether to trust that judgment now or just chalk his feelings up as the most normal sort of nervous wonder anyone might have before stepping off into the unknown. He tells himself that this night is going to be like a lot of things in his life that have already come and gone with no terrible after-effects. Once he gets going and everything is in motion he will be fine and dandy like he's always been before, like he is planning to always be in the future.

"I thought we were going to the drive-in," Ann says when he gets back in the car. He's left the radio on for her to listen to while he went inside, and he notices she has turned up the volume a little. The Chiffons are on singing 'Sweet Talking Guy.' "I don't really care if we do or not. It's not like I'm that crazy to see 'King Kong Meets Godzilla.'"

"I don't think it's going to win an academy award anytime soon," Ray says. "If you want to we can just ride around for a while."

"I'd like that." She looks at the paper bag Ray brings from under the seat, a small smile coming to her face. "What have you got there?"

"I picked you up a little present on my way over."

"Let me see."

She pulls the bottle from the bag and looks at the label.

"Sipping whiskey?" she asks. "I've never had anything like that before. A few of my friends had some wine we stole from somebody's parents' house one time, but not enough to really get drunk. We just got a little silly is all that happened."

"There's enough in that bottle to get you a whole lot more than silly. I'll guarantee you that." He stops the car at a stop sign in some quiet neighborhood off the main highway. He doesn't particularly want to hear Ann protesting the strength of the way he's mixed the whiskey in her fountain drink, but he doesn't feel like messing around and missing his chance either, so he goes ahead and sloshes a good portion in and swishes it around. He hands it to her and smiles, then lifts the bottle and takes a long straight drink. It doesn't gag him or surprise him like it had first done the night before, but there is still a kick anyway. He breathes out deeply like he has just finished a half mile run and motions for her to take a sip.

"Go ahead," he says. "See if you like it."

She tastes the contents and makes a short gasping sound when she swallows, but that doesn't stop her from trying it again. Ray drives for a while with the radio on and tells her what he had done last night and today and all this week of Easter vacation. He asks her about school and what she does and doesn't like about it, which teachers she hates and if she is thinking of going to college two years down the line. Most of what he has to say he is astonished to see is witty and charming and infinitely humorous, because after a time he feels he has Ann's rapt attention to his stories and is aware of how she is hanging on his every word as she leans back in her seat and smiles and drinks from the Burger Chef cup that he keeps filling every time they stop.

It is after an hour or so of driving that he suddenly feels the need to pull the Super Sport over and turn the key off and let the engine rest for a spell. It is uncomfortable trying to slither over the console and the shifter in the middle between the bucket seats, so he finally abandons all such gymnastic procedures and gets out of the car and walks to the other side. They are parked on a dark road overlooking a railroad track by a wire fence where on down the way is a pasture where sometimes bulls and cows can be spotted chewing cuds and eating grass. Now in the darkness he can't tell if there are any farm animals about, nor can he see farmers with guns who might think he and Ann are trespassing on their private property. With the whiskey in him as it is, he can safely say he doesn't truly care who or what is out there now.

"Why don't we take a walk?" he says.

He takes her hand and helps her out of the car, surprising himself at how gentle he is in grasping her hand when there is such a fire burning within him and his every impulse is to hurry. He thinks of how long it seems he has been waiting for this night and he wants to go about doing what he needs to do to make it special, but he also feels the desire to take his time and not rush it and make it somehow last, because he knows that once this moment inside this night is done it will be gone from him forever.

He wonders if other boys on their way to being men thought this same way he does now, and he doesn't know what the answer is. A part of him doubts it, and he doesn't know whether to feel superior or to be ashamed of himself for living in his mind so much and not being a creature of the flesh like everybody else who is normal. He thinks of his Uncle Jack and wonders if he has ever harbored such thoughts in his head. He knows his dad hasn't, nor his brother or Jimmy or any other male he knows of. He wonders if being this way is going to make him strange and weird for the rest of his life, and if he is always going to have to be careful not to let anyone know what he is thinking too much. But then, anyway, he is really that way most of the time now already.

They come to a place where the winding path takes an even deeper curve and stops at a clearing to a dark place surrounded by spring thickets and early-flowering trees. In the pocket of an opportune grove he holds Ann in his arms and kisses her slowly and fully with hardly a star to light his way. Ray wonders how he knows so expertly what he is doing, how his lips and hands know where to go with each heartbeat and breath, and it comes to his mind that this moment isn't anything like what he has thought it would be. There is no rushing and hurrying and telling himself he has to do something at such a time and follow it up with something else. There is not a question or a worry within him whether he is doing something totally right or absolutely wrong and if later on he will hate himself or Ann Caldwell will hate him or laugh at him or go and tell everyone how inept and wrong he had been; but it is nothing like that now. It is all like it is a dream and he doesn't know how it is going to go but he does not want it to end so fast.

It is like that totally.

And that is when he knows he doesn't want to do what anybody else would do right now. He doesn't want to take Ann Caldwell back to the Super Sport and lay her down in the back seat and go at her like so many before him have done on nights like this, on back roads with no traffic or light to make things stop. He doesn't want to do it because it is so easy to go ahead and do such an act, because it is what everyone else has done and is doing most nights and will do in the future, and he doesn't want to be with them or like them. He doesn't want to be one of them and have to sit around and talk about it later and grin. It is not that way for him now and never has been and he knows it.

It is not long before he comes to the realization that Ann Caldwell shares none of the thoughts and feelings that are flashing and sweeping through his mind. He feels her pushing herself against him, pulling him closer with each hot April breath, and he has a sudden gap in his thinking when she takes his hand and places it upon her. He feels her breasts and she guides his hand down the top of her dress, and he knows what she wants him to do without a doubt. There is a moment he is sure he can no longer pull away or maintain any wherewithal of traveling down a road no one else is on, and he wonders if this is the way it always is, if a person just says things to themselves and decides things according to the way they think they should be and then throws their words and resolutions away just as quickly as spitting out something that didn't taste so good after all, no matter how good it might be for you. He kisses her back hard and rough, and he lets his hands run over her fast and dirty and as wild as the flowers shooting up through the soil.

But just when he believes he is lost forever in this forest he comes back to himself again. Somehow he sees her face in a slither of moonlight and stars and there is something there that holds him up, that tells him to slow himself and look even closer at what he thinks he's seen. There is a trickle of sweat in a tiny pool on the ridge above her lips, and he feels oily greasy makeup sticking to his face. Her hair is not so buoyant or cascading, but hangs in small strings on her forehead, like something used and leftover and fake from some cheap holiday celebration that has never meant a thing. She is not so desirable or magnificent at all, this Ann Caldwell, he decides. She is not so much as he has cranked her up to be. He wonders how he can detach himself from her now, how he can get her back to the car and to her own home without any further masquerading or self-deception, and how, once she is gone from him tonight he can make it so he will never see or think of her again, because he knows if he does he will give up on it all. He will never be able to play any such game as this ever again.

There are lights coming down the road that help Ray to stop with his hands and his thoughts and instead look out from their thicket and see who is coming. When he sees the police cruiser pull up beside his car he has the sinking feeling his lucky streak is over, so he begins thinking of excuses and alibis he can offer to explain his presence on this dark road within this forest with a pretty girl and a bottle of whiskey. Speaking of the whiskey, he looks down and sees the bottle leaning against a tree, a sight which makes him thankful unto God he's remembered to bring it along for his and Ann's moonlight stroll. He reaches down and picks it up and chucks it off into the bushes. He puts a finger to his lips and tells Ann, "Sshhh."

There are two policemen. One walks around the Super Sport looking in the windows with a flashlight while the other stays in the patrol car and plays with the radio. Ray can hear the static and the sound of voices coming through the open window while he wonders just exactly what to do next.

"We're going to have to go out and talk to these guys," he tells Ann. "Let me do the talking if you can, and for god's sake try and act like you haven't been drinking anything. Smile a lot and agree with everything they say."

"Hey, officer," Ray says as he and Ann come toward the Super Sport. "We heard you drive up."

The cop by the car makes certain to shine his flashlight directly in Ray's face so that Ray has to freeze in his tracks to keep from tripping over anything. This action, he thinks, might be a blessing in disguise, since walking and taking steps in front of these two policemen might not be the best way to present himself and Ann right at the moment. It might be best to just stand still here in the road and smile like he is happy to have the local law enforcement agency make an appearance.

"Is this your car?"

"Yes, sir."

"What are you two doing out here?"

The first thing that crosses Ray's mind is to weave an elaborate lie to explain his parked 1963 Chevrolet Super Sport and his and Ann's presence in the dark of the woods on a spring night, but thinking better of it he reaches back in his head and decides to do something totally off the board and tell the truth, or at least tell the truth as far as he wants to go with it. There are a few details he thinks might be best to omit.

"Well, sir, I'll tell you." He looks at the policeman and watches his partner get out from behind the wheel of the cruiser. My, he thinks, what big pistols they have. He wonders what Uncle Jack would do in a situation like this. He thinks maybe he knows.

"I just got this car the day before yesterday," he explains. It is like Uncle Jack's voice is doing the explaining and not his. "I hadn't had this car a day before somebody stole it and took it for a joyride. I haven't had the chance to even show it to my girlfriend here until tonight, because I've been working every day and we both had to go to church earlier tonight and this is the first chance I've had to show it to her. After we got out of church we decided to go for a ride. After a while I got tired of driving, so I drove up here and parked. I'm not going to lie to you. I was wanting to come up here and maybe make out a little, but now you guys have shown up, so it looks like that isn't going to happen."

"What about you?" the first officer says to Ann. "Did you come up here to make out too?"

"No, sir," Ann says, cool as hell. "I thought we were going for a walk."

"I remember this car from the reports the other day," the second officer says. "You're lucky to get it back so fast."

"I know," Ray says. "I thought it was gone for good, along with my life savings."

"It's a nice car," the first officer says. "You ought to know better than to park it on a road like this. Somebody'll come along and hit it."

Ray doesn't answer, just stands and shakes his head and tries to look dumber than he really is.

"You two get in and get out of here," the officer says. "Don't let us catch you up here again. We're letting you go this time with a warning. Only reason I'm not giving you a ticket is because you told the truth about what you were doing. Anyway, I've seen you before. You work down at that used car lot on Main. I've seen you washing cars out there sometimes."

"Yes, sir," Ray smiles. "That's me all right."

"Go on then."

Ray holds on to Ann's elbow, helping her take careful plodding steps so she won't fall down in front of the two policemen and cause the jig to be up. Ann is trying to smile, but Ray can tell she is scared sober now and wants to get away from here and back to her house as fast as she can.

"I think I need to go home now, if you don't mind," she tells him when they drive away. "I'm not feeling too good."

"You're not going to be sick, are you?"

"No," she says. "I'll be okay."

"That's good," Ray says. What he doesn't say is, if she isn't okay and is going to be sick, then could she please stick her head out the window and throw her guts up there instead of inside his car on the nice clean carpet?

He'll appreciate it if she can do that little favor for him. She can be sure he will never ask her for anything ever again.

And boy, does he mean never.

~~~~~

Jack can't remember the last time he's felt like this, but it has been a while and he's hoped such sensations were things of the past and he wouldn't have to have such trepidations jumping around in his head again. But the truth of it is he didn't quite know what to do right this minute. Usually he was cool and even-minded and events of the world didn't matter that much to him, but somehow this night everything seems to have escalated and formed into one big problematic mess that he is having trouble shaking.

He turns the corner in the Eldorado and looks in his mirror to see if anyone has turned behind him, and when he is convinced there is no one following his car he relaxes for just a minute and tries to decide exactly what he should do.

It isn't that he hasn't had somebody after him before. He'd dealt with jealous boyfriends and husbands more than once during his time, so it isn't like this is anything new. He knows how to deal with situations when there is bad blood and jealousy involved. A lot of times all a fellow had to do was put a little distance between the other guy and the passage of time and the varying tides of passion and emotion would ebb before any harm was done. Jack has learned that most people don't really want trouble; they just like to run their mouths and say a lot of big words and get the feeling inside themselves that somebody in the world has heard what they'd said and took note of it and was duly impressed, but the notion of actually doing something drastic and life changing and negatively noteworthy was generally out of the question and only reserved for movies and blockbuster novels where nobody truly acted the way real people do.

So that was the way it had always been before, but this time it is different. There is a bullet hole in the back taillight of the Caddy to attest to that fact. Jack can't believe Marie Corlew's ex-husband could resort to shooting at him just because Jack had seen Marie a few nights here lately. And the bad thing about it is Marie's ex-husband is Chuck, and Chuck and he have been drinking buddies for at least twenty years. It isn't like he's cheating with Marie on Chuck, because, goddamn, they'd been divorced at least three years now, so why all of a sudden is Chuck getting so upset about him and Marie being out together while Jack is in town on vacation and wants to take his pistol out and blow somebody's head off because of it?

The thing is Chuck knows where the motel is Jack is staying at, and he knows where Loretta's house is and what kind of car Jack is driving and just about everything else too. It isn't like Jack could go spend the night with his sister or go back to his motel room and get his stuff and clear out back to Clarksville a few days early, because then he might as well go back home and hide out forever like a goddamn coward. He could, of course, go to the police and let them know what is going on, tell them how somebody has taken a shot at him and winged his Cadillac, but the idea of getting the law all involved in some little spat that had risen a bit out of control seems like much ado about almost nothing, although it isn't nothing that has him afraid of Chuck and what he might do and where Chuck might go to find him, and so he is driving around trying to think how he could possibly get a handle on all this bullshit that had started out as only a few nights of fun on this vacation trip to Nashville.

Damn it, Jack thinks. Here it is Thursday night and I haven't done half of what I wanted to. I was going to the Opry tomorrow night and Saturday too. I've got tickets back at the room and now I'm wondering if I'm even going to be around to get to use them. Now ain't that a crock of shit?

He keeps driving and thinking. It is going to be a damn shame if he has to cut his vacation short over something stupid like this.

~~~~~

Good Friday begins for Ray with some bird who could have been a pterodactyl squawking from a branch outside his window, sounding like he is sitting on the bedpost even though he is ten yards away with the window closed. Perhaps it is that the bird is not truly that loud or ear-piercing as it sounds, but in Ray's weakened morning state the tweeting permeates his eardrum and travels directly to his tender brain like a Gemini rocket from Cape

Kennedy. He tries ignoring it for five minutes or so, but gives up after some particularly trilly renderings and sits up in the bed to massage his head and see if the possibility exists it might stop pounding. He doesn't have a whole lot of hope.

He'd been more than glad to deposit Ann Caldwell back at her doorstep last night, not just because the romantic interlude between them had been shattered or because the addition of Jack Daniel's into her system had transformed her previously desirable form into something Ray was more than willing to not regard or pursue any longer, but mainly because he found himself cooling off prematurely and wishing in a private sort of way that he could be rid and done with the Anns and Jimmys of the world for a spell or two and go along his merry way with only the company of his car and himself. He had wondered momentarily if he was indeed becoming strange and perhaps turning weird, but after getting rid of Ann and driving around for a few hours listening to the radio and killing off the procured bottle of Jack Daniel's he'd decided that the reason he preferred his own company on a moonlit night in April instead of being with a female the likes of Ann that every other guy he knew of would kill to intertwine with was because he was different from all the rest of them and it was better for him to be away from the crowd and all they had to offer for a time while he took note of his status and pondered his existence and figured out precisely what in the hell he ought to do to get along in this world that a huge percentage of himself didn't want to be a part of.

He wants to eat breakfast before he has to be at work, so he walks out on the porch and down the steps to his car. It isn't until he opens the door to get in that he sees Uncle Jack in the backseat curled up with his jacket covering his shoulders. He thinks for a minute Jack is asleep, but then he sees his eyes are open and a funny smile is on his face.

"What are you doing here?" Ray asks.

"Up until a minute ago I was trying to get a little sleep, but I have to say it hasn't worked out that good for me." Jack sits up and takes the jacket off his arms, holds it up and looks at it to see how badly it is wrinkled. "This is a good size backseat you have here but it really isn't made for sleeping. Maybe one or two of Snow White's dwarfs could curl up and get comfortable for the night, but a guy like me doesn't stand a chance stretching out back here."

"How come you're sleeping in my car? Where's your Cadillac?"

"The Cadillac is at this moment parked at City Hall, about a mile or so from here. I left it there about three this morning and hiked over here to spend the night. I didn't want to wake anybody up, so I just bedded down out here for the night."

Jack can see Ray looking at him, so he gets out of the car and stretches and lights a cigarette. He's been wanting a cigarette off and on for a while, but he thought it was bad manners to smoke in somebody else's car when they weren't around. Cars, after all, were holy to a lot of folks, just like the Caddy is holy to him, is his most prized possession and all that jazz, and he figured it is the same way with Ray and this Chevy too. Heck, the kid is just like him in so many other ways—it would be only natural for Ray to treasure a big hunk of gleaming metal too.

"I had a little trouble with a fellow last night, Ray," he tells him. "Maybe I ought not to let you in on all the gory details, but the fact of the matter is this fellow had a pistol and took a couple of shots at me. He got pissed off because I had a date or two with his ex-wife, which I don't get at all. He wanted to kill me over somebody he wasn't even married to anymore. Hell, if you ask me, it's not worth killing anybody in a case like this even if the woman and the guy are still married. I know I sure as hell wouldn't get involved, but then, I've never been married. Maybe I don't understand how things work."

"Do you think he's still after you?" Ray asks. He looks up and down the street to see if anybody is coming.

"Could be. I don't really know." Jack takes a pensive draw from the cigarette and shakes his head. "I thought for a while he was following me last night. I was afraid to go back to my place because I thought he might be waiting for me. I figured he might get over it with a good night's sleep. He was pretty damned drunk. So was I, as a matter of fact."

"What are you going to do now?"

"I guess I'll go back and get my car, if you'll give me a ride. Then I'll try to figure out what to do next." Jack sighs and squints up at the sun, looking disgusted as hell. "I hate to act like a chicken and go home," he says. "Hell, I've got tickets to the Opry tonight and tomorrow."

Ray doesn't say much about that, but just gets in the car and starts up the engine. He can't see why going to the Opry is all that important. Heck, it's country music, that's all. It isn't like it's rock and roll.

"Come on," he says. "I'll take you to your car."

~~~~~

The thing that disgusts him the most is that he's told himself he would never find himself in this kind of a fix ever again, yet here he is. The last time it was like this was three years ago back home in Clarksville, when he'd had that husband come to the Trailways office looking for him. That had been bad enough. Granted, the guy hadn't had a gun on him or anything like that, but it was still a hell of a thing to have an altercation going on right where you made your living. He'd been able to fend the husband off—had even been able to punch him a couple of times and slam him into a wall to hold him at bay and calm him down, but it still didn't do much to keep his boss and the front office very satisfied with his goings on after hours. He'd had to call the union in on that one to keep from getting fired or suspended, and the result was he was on probation for a couple of months and had to watch his every step for a while for fear of getting canned. Women weren't worth all this trouble, he'd told himself then. A good-paying job with great benefits was hard to come by, so a sacrifice was going to have to be made. He was going to have to cut out all this wild shit that seemed to want to follow him around. He was going to have to be a good boy and tone things down.

And he'd done good for a while. He'd cut back on his drinking and made it a habit to stay away from some of those venues where he tended to get in trouble, bars and joints and casinos and such, and he told himself to keep his trousers on as much as possible when he met a strange woman—and especially if he met a woman who he knew was attached to some form of husband or boyfriend. The way he had it figured was there were plenty of women around for a guy with his attributes, single and not bad looking and bursting with personality with a good job and ready money to go with it. He didn't have to take chances and ride in the gutters so much like he had as a young man, but old habits were hard to stop, so he really had to work at it. He'd managed to keep his demons at bay for a good stint now, but now he's come into Nashville and made the mistake of visiting some old haunts and meeting up with a few old wild drinking partners from the service days, and the next thing he knew he was hitting on Marie Corlew at the Orchid Lounge, and he should have known somehow it would get back to Chuck. Hell, he knew Chuck from way back, and he knew just how Chuck was. If Marie was married to him once then it didn't matter one whit if they were divorced or not, because she was still his no matter what the courts had to say about it. Jack had that fact in the back of his head the whole time he began fooling around with Marie, but he had gone ahead and done it anyway. He threw every learned lesson and all his caution to the wind. And why? Because once upon a time—what was it, ten or twelve years ago?—he'd looked Marie over once and decided how one day he wouldn't mind getting into her pants.

So he had. He's not only gotten into her pants but he's done it time and time again over the past three days. Hell, he's probably set a record for an old guy like him, like he is making up for lost time after the couple of years he's scaled back and tried to be a good boy for a while. And now he has Chuck Corlew after him, brandishing a goddamn gun the last time he'd seen him, taking a frigging shot at the Cadillac like they are all back in the War again. This is the kind of shit he can definitely do without.

The Caddy is just like he had left it during the early morning hours. The Goodlettsville police haven't towed it in for being parked at City Hall and Chuck Corlew hasn't come across it and pumped all the ammunition in his pistol into the tires and the body, so Jack tosses his worries aside and goes down to the motel to see if anyone is waiting for him. All appears to be quiet, so he goes across the street and has breakfast, then comes back and catches a little shuteye for a while. He isn't a young man anymore. He needs a little sleep every now and then or he has trouble adding two and two together.

When he wakes up he can tell it is early afternoon by the way the sun's rays slant against the shades by the room's only window. He gets up and sits on the side of the bed for a minute, toying with the feeling in his chest that he had better be ready and prepared for what this night has to offer. A part of him says to get his things together right now and go and check out and go back to Clarksville before the sun starts to set, but there is also that part of him that says if he does that he might as well fold all his cards forever and go check in at an old age home where everybody makes all his decisions for him, because he is effectively announcing that he isn't a man anymore and he can't take care of what life throws at him like he had when he was young and virile and nothing scared him whatsoever, not even the barrel of a gun. He isn't going to start spending the rest of his life with his tail tucked between his legs. Not today at least, that's for sure. Not in the middle of a vacation he's been looking forward to for a while. And not in front of the only family he has left in the world, who'd all want to know why he'd beat it out of town so fast and hadn't come by for Easter dinner.

But he still has that feeling inside him. He feels the urge to stop traveling the road he is going down and turn off in another direction and leave the events and circumstances of this life to someone else. Let somebody else worry about Marie and Chuck Corlew from now on, and let him move on down the highway to something far more pleasant. It wouldn't be a crime for him to leave this all behind, now would it?

He looks at his satchel and his suitcase lying on the dresser, and the temptation to take off fills him almost to the gills, threatening to overflow in his body and turn him into a quivering mass of jelly. He doesn't like this unfamiliar feeling of being frightened, of huddling in a strange darkened motel room miles from home and quaking like a little boy getting ready to receive his first spanking. What is he, a little baby? He's been to war. He's been threatened and shot at and had people after him before. This is nothing new. He doesn't know what in the hell is wrong with him. He is just going to have to be a man and face this shit down. He'll be all right. He's had worse stuff than this come at him before.

~ ~ ~ ~ ~

He has an extra ticket to the Friday night Opry, but Jack is damned if he is going to call Marie Corlew and see if she wants to go, even if it does mean he might not have a partner in bed later in the night. Of course, what with the events of Thursday night he shouldn't even be thinking of going to the Opry or even be in town any longer than it takes to start the Cadillac and hit the city limits, but the stubborn side of him has kicked in good now, and he's talked himself into sticking around town as planned and leaving Easter afternoon after dinner at Loretta's. Sure, maybe he is taking a chance not leaving, but there is something in him that doesn't much cotton to the idea that somebody has run him out of town. He hasn't been afraid of anybody or anything for a lot of years now, and damned if he is going to start acting that way now. There isn't anybody who could scare him into doing something he doesn't want to and there isn't a soul on the face of the earth who is going to tell him how to live his life. I'll tell them just what I've always told everybody, he thinks. I'm going to live until I die. You'd think everybody would be used to that idea by now. But some people are slow learners.

He doesn't much feel like hitting town until later, so he walks out the door, and, after checking the Cadillac for additional bullet holes and determining that no further damage has occurred during his nap, he drives over the bridge north to a barbecue restaurant he always makes it a point to visit when he is in Nashville. It is just beginning to get dark when he arrives, and for a moment he debates letting the top down on the Caddy and coming back outside to eat in the car while he watches the stars come out and the planes fly over from Berry Field Airport; but because of the neighborhood and the influx of characters and winos and homeless vagrants he decides that is probably not the wisest thing he could do, so he locks the car and goes inside to eat.

For a good while he sits in a booth by the cash register up front and looks out the window at the traffic going back and forth from town. There doesn't seem to be as much action for this Friday night as he remembers there being in the past, but he reasons that the lack of traffic on the streets and the few customers inside the restaurant with him has something to do with the fact that this is Good Friday. A lot of people are off work today, so maybe they are at home or gone out of town. It could be a lot of churches are having services to commemorate this day when Jesus got crucified, so maybe that has something to do with how quiet it is. But there is something about the silence that doesn't jive with that reasoning for him. The silence of the city isn't about it being a religious moment or people being away from their jobs and their homes. It is something completely different than that. No, it is the silence of waiting in anticipation, of knowing something is in the air and on the way and when it comes and makes its entrance nothing will be the same again. Jack finds himself straining his eyes out the window, then looking down at his hands and all his possessions gathered on the surface of the table. He looks at his keys, his pack of Luckies, the Zippo lighter he's carried with him since he was a kid. It seems like a meager collection for a fellow his age. You would think he might have a little more to show than this. It is like something is missing and he can't put his finger on what it is.

He has the extra ticket in his pocket and he looks at the pay phone on the wall five feet away. He reaches in his pocket for a dime and dials Loretta's number hoping against hope she or Albert don't answer. He hopes it isn't late enough that Ray has already left the house for the evening. It is only a little past six. Surely he won't be gone this soon.

It is John who answers the phone. Jack has to act like he is glad to talk to his oldest nephew and that this is the reason he's phoned on a Friday night, but after a few minutes of pleasantries there is little more to say, so Jack asks if Ray is around because he wants to tell him something about his car, and in a minute Ray is on the other end of the line.

"What are you doing tonight?" Jack asks.

"I don't know," Ray says. "I was fixing to call somebody and see if anything was going on. I could have had a date with a girl, but I decided I didn't want to."

"I could have had a date too," Jack grins, "but I thought it was just too dangerous to go through with it." He wonders if Ray got the joke, and, if he did, why he wasn't laughing. "Hey, I was wondering if you might want to go downtown with me tonight. I've got an extra ticket to the Friday Night Opry."

"Country music? I don't know, Uncle Jack."

"Aw, it's the same as rock and roll once you get up close to it. That's where old Elvis came from. Jerry Lee Lewis. They've all got guitars and pianos and such. They just play them a little bit differently."

"Do I have to wear a straw hat and overalls?"

"Hell, boy, you can go in your birthday suit if you want."

He pays for his sandwich and leaves a good tip on the table, even though his waitress was fat and ugly as hell and took her time about bringing him a second beer. In the lot the Cadillac sat red and shiny and sticking out like hell from all the other heaps and bombs and scrappy cars parked around it. Once again he thinks about putting the top down so Ray could get the full effect of the car and the night on the way downtown, but then he thinks of Loretta and Albert looking out the window and seeing him in their driveway. He thinks of John and Brenda seeing their brother ride off with him in the Cadillac with the radio playing, and he knows if it is that way he'll have to come up with something to make it right with all of them later on. Maybe with the top up the fact that he's chosen Ray to go won't come across so noticeable, and maybe later on it won't come down so hard on Ray for being the chosen one of Jack Patterson, like it means there is something wrong and bad about him too.

Ray is sitting in the porch swing waiting when Jack pulls up, so there isn't any need to get out and go in and chew the fat with anybody for a while. Actually, Ray tells him, there isn't anybody home but John, and he is taking a bath. Brenda is spending the night with a friend, and Loretta and Albert are at the grocery store. They back out and drive up the street to turn right and go back to Nashville. Jack gives the Caddy a little gas so Ray could see his Super Sport isn't the only car in the family that has a big engine.

"Look in that glove box in front of you and see if you can find something that might wet our whistles a little." Jack glances over and watches Ray pull the paper bag out and take the Jack Daniel's bottle out and hold it up and look at it. "I've got a little flask we'll fill up before we go in. It'll make you appreciate country music a whole lot more once you learn how to listen to it."

He looks over at his nephew breaking the seal on the bottle. It isn't that Jack wants to lead him down the wrong path or put him in a situation where his life might go to shit, but there is still a part of him that wants Ray to enjoy himself and see what else life has to offer beyond all of Loretta's world of rules and regulations and boundaries and a long future of lifelessness with never a laugh or a smile anywhere to be found. It isn't like he is being a criminal and being a bad influence on a minor or anything like that. Hell, he just wants Ray to be happy and have a good full life. It is something Jack can give to him besides money. It is a form of love Loretta and Albert don't know a damn thing about. Jack thinks it is a sin to keep it from a fellow just right there on the cusp.

"I don't generally suggest drinking that stuff straight," Jack advises. "It's a whole lot safer mixing it with a little water. But when you're out on the road I guess you just have to make do one way or the other."

They pass the bottle back and forth a few times at red lights and stop signs. On the radio Flatt and Scruggs play "Foggy Mountain Breakdown". They are real popular right now because of that Bonnie and Clyde movie that is out. Jack has given some thought to going and seeing it, but he hasn't yet. He hasn't been to a movie since "Psycho". That has been a while back.

It is still an hour before the show starts, so Jack looks for a good parking slot to leave the Caddy, finding a good place within walking distance of the bars between there and the Ryman Auditorium. It is a damn shame, he thinks. Here his nephew lives within a half hour's drive from the Opry and he's never even been. If you ask him, Loretta and Albert have neglected this boy's education in a big way. They've had the boy going to church every time the door got opened from the time he was out of diapers, but they've never done anything to show him anything else in life that might have been the slightest bit of fun. Look at what they'd accomplished with John, three years older than Ray. Jack has never seen a more boring son of a bitch than him. Never had done the first thing wrong, straight A's on his report cards, no staying out late or having anything to do with what Jack thought were the finer things in life at all, and now there he was four hours away in Knoxville acting like he was a holy monk when there was opportunity in abundance everywhere a fellow could look. What a waste, Jack thinks. If he'd had the chance to be somewhere like that when he was nineteen things would have been different, and he can't keep from hoping Ray feels the same way when it is his time to get out into the world.

He fills the flask and the two of them walk down the big hill by the river toward the bars on Broad. There are massage parlors and men drinking and bumming money at every block crossing, and Jack tries to keep walking at a

Super Sport

good pace so that maybe Ray won't have to actually get elbow to elbow with any of the riff-raff. There are a lot of whores and crazy con artists around, and Jack is pretty sure Ray hasn't come across too much of this sort in the life he's been leading up until this week. It is probably a good idea not to baptize the boy in too deep a river right off the bat and all at once. There is such a thing as taking it a little at a time.

He knows of one bar where he is pretty sure he and Ray can sit down and have a couple of beers without a lot of trouble. Ray doesn't exactly look like he is twenty-one and legal much, but this bar, Johnny Ace's, isn't exactly the most law-abiding place in town either. Jack is confident the last thing anybody inside would be worried about is whether the kid with him is legal or not. Hell, he has a five dollar bill in his pocket that will take care of that.

They have two Lone Star Drafts, then another each for the road. Ray wants to pour a little whiskey in his glass to make it a boilermaker like he's read about somewhere but Jack tells him no and won't pass him the flask.

"It's still pretty early," Jack tells him. "I'm afraid you're going to peak too soon."

Jack hands over a ten dollar bill to the waitress and tells her to keep the change just so he can see her smile. She is a pretty little thing about twenty-three or so, and if Ray wasn't with him he'd probably do something like come back after the show and see how available she might be, but it is time now to go to the Ryman because the show is starting, so off they go across the street and down the walk and back up the hill a ways. Jack has been drinking a fairly good while and he is feeling pretty good now.

They listen to George Hamilton IV sing "Abeline" and watch Jeannie Seely sing three songs, the best of which was "Don't Touch Me," which both Jack and Ray really like. Jack likes the looks of Jeannie Seely while Ray is at the point where he likes anything. When Jack Greene comes out and

98

sings "There Goes My Everything" Ray stands up and applauds like it is the greatest thing he's ever heard. Jack keeps looking at him and wondering if he ought to keep the flask away from him for a little while. After a while Ray gets that look on his face that says he's probably had enough for a while, and the next thing Jack knows he is watching his nephew haul himself off at a good clip to make it into one of the restrooms and get rid of the majority of his dinner. Jack has to give the young man credit though; in a matter of minutes Ray is back in his seat and clapping for each song and telling his uncle it is time to pass the flask again.

The first show ends and Jack wonders if there is enough interest left in Ray to stay for the second. Perhaps it isn't a matter of interest but is instead of an endurance factor—would Ray be able to stay enough on the sober side that he might be able to exit the auditorium at the end of the second show and also be ambulatory enough to make it a few blocks down the way to the Eldorado? Jack isn't so sure. And he also wonders if by tempting fate and remaining in the building if an arrest for Drunk and Disorderly might not be too far off in the future? God, his sister would kill him over something like that.

It isn't the best time Ray has ever had in his life, but it isn't bad. It is better than a lot of stuff he's gone through lately, and he has this feeling there is more of this to come after tonight, as long as he stays close to his uncle. He feels like he's turned a corner with Uncle Jack over the last few days; he feels like he's finally met up with somebody in his family he can relate to and who might in some strange way understand where he is coming from. Up until this week he has always been inclined to believe there is no one anywhere in his family he could possibly talk to who might give the first damn about what he is saying. He is trying to tell himself that the fact Uncle Jack has come through with money toward his Super Sport doesn't really elevate him a mile or two ahead of everybody else in the family, but it is still nice of his uncle to do something like that for him when it would have been just as easy to keep the money and spend it on himself. Ray isn't sure what he feels about this gift of giving. He's never experienced it before from his dad or mom or anyone else, and now out of the blue here his uncle comes from another city and with no strings attached buys him a car. Was his uncle like everybody else Ray knows, and just doing something so he could get something out of it later? And now here he was supplying him with liquor and taking him to the Friday night Opry—what is Ray supposed to think about all that? It is like he wants to trust his uncle but is afraid to. He doesn't trust anybody else he knows and hasn't for the longest time now, so it is pretty hard to make an exception for Uncle Jack, even if he does have a new car and a bellyful of whiskey that he's never even been near to having only a few days ago.

It has been a strange week so far.

"The second show is just like the first," Jack says. "We can stay and see it again if you want."

"I'm all right either way, Uncle Jack. Whatever you want to do is fine."

"We might need to get out and get you some air. You're beginning to look a little green around the gills to me."

"I'm feeling better now. I just swallowed when I should have been breathing. I got a little choked up."

"It happens to the best of us."

They walk down a long stairway to get to the street. Jack watches to make sure Ray is holding on to the rail and isn't going to fall down and break his neck. He is surprised at how steady the boy is and how he navigates down without a care or the first show of concern, and he has to marvel at how recuperative youth is and how fast a boy can recover from something that would fell a bull elephant of a man for all the next day just like that. Jack tries to remember how it was when he was a kid and could go all night, but it is getting to be a long time now and he is having more and more trouble recollecting such scenes. It seems to him right then that thoughts like this are coming more and more often these days. Pretty soon he'll be longing for the good old days all the time.

A light rain starts to fall and Jack makes sure he is careful in his steps so he won't slip on the wet sidewalk and fall and bust his ass in front of Ray. He isn't sure if it is so, but he would like to think that the boy might have some kind of hero worship thing going for him as of now, seeing how he's put wheels beneath him and introduced him to a side of life the boy has only dreamed of ever experiencing. He'd like to think that Ray genuinely likes him, that he doesn't regard his uncle as another tiresome full of shit adult who is always coming along and getting in his way and trying to tell him how to live his life without once considering that he might know how already. Lord, Jack thinks, listen to me. I think I'm the one who needs to worry about having too much to drink.

"Let's stop in here and have another beer," he says when they get to Johnny Ace's. "Maybe in a few minutes the rain will stop and we won't get drenched getting to the car."

He is trying not to dwell too much on the idea of seeing the little waitress he'd given the big tip to a couple of hours ago, but when they walk through the door he immediately begins looking for where she is and if she is still working the same section as before. Ray is smiling at him and rubbing the water out of his hair with his hand.

"Shit, you don't fool me at all, Uncle Jack. You just want to see that woman who brought us our drinks again."

"I never could put one by on you, could I?"

When he spots her with her back to them at the end of the bar Jack walks over to the nearest table and sits down. Ray makes his way over to a Rockola in the corner and studies what is on it. He leans on the glass and looks at the names, wondering exactly how long he can stand here before he starts sliding to the floor. The names are all blurs and he doesn't have any coins on him anyway. He'll have to get change at the bar and the bar is a long way off. He isn't so sure he can make it. He is drunk. Boy, is he drunk. He's been trying not to show it and to keep it hid, but he isn't so sure he can do it anymore. He is already way past that now.

He drifts to the table where his uncle and the waitress are talking, getting a smile from her as he sits down and tries to look the least bit sober. He doesn't know if it is working or not, but nobody says anything and that is good. He watches the waitress walk away and wonders if she is married and what she looks like naked. His mind, it seems, is drag racing all over the place now, speeding up like the Super Sport does when he punches the accelerator. He is really going to have to watch it now. He can tell something is up by the way Uncle Jack is looking at him.

"I told her to bring you a Coke," Jack smiles. "I think maybe you've had enough for one night. You're about to go around the bend."

Ray doesn't argue with him, so Jack knows he is right. Probably this hasn't been the greatest idea he'd ever had, bringing the boy along and letting him get his fill of whiskey and beer not only tonight but all week long too, but Jack had felt that blue lonesome feeling come over him back at the motel and in the back seat of Ray's Chevy last night, and even though he tried to talk himself out of it he still knew it had him by the shorthairs and there wasn't any escaping it if he tried facing it alone. It came over him that way from time to time. It didn't have to make an appearance by having somebody shoot at him, but that incident with Chuck Corlew didn't help keep it away either. Sometimes the blue lonesomes would come and find him even when he was right in the middle of laughing it up or having a good time or in bed with a new piece of tail. When it was his time he couldn't get away from it. He'd even stopped trying to these days, just saw it coming and waited up for it and let it wash over him.

"You all right?" Ray asks.

Jack nods his head, looking at the boy as if he is seeing him at last. He is so young, so full of that thing Jack has always had and wanted to always hold on to, yet there is something in this studying of his nephew that causes him to frown a little, to know that all this youth and fullness and anticipation for what is to come will one day slow and still and settle into what Jack feels residing in him lately. No woman will be pretty enough, no bottle strong enough, no car fast and flashy enough to keep forever. There will always be a time for trade-ins on everything, the women, the cars, the places to go, and as the months and years pass those trade-ins, that bartering for something new and uplifting, will beg for attention more frequently, until finally all there would be was each new day becoming a quest to leave what was in the day before behind. Like it had become for him— and he admitted it now right here—it would become for Ray. The world would become less new. Everything he saw he would have already seen before.

The thing of it, Jack notes, is he is feeling this way and he isn't the least bit morose and he for damned sure isn't truly all that drunk either. He could buy three more bottles and guzzle them down one after another and he would be no more intoxicated after that than he is now. He watches Ray wobble along singing and he envies him this moment.

"There goes my reason for living," Ray sings. "There goes my everything."

Jack smiles only a trace, thinking how he would never sing like this again. The songs are all Ray's now; Jack doesn't feel any melodies inside him, forcing their way out of his lungs in an effort to escape into the air, out into the heavens above. He will miss that, he thinks. It is not going to be any fun being an old man who's forgotten how to sing.

They arrive at the Cadillac and Jack walks around to the driver's side, running his hand along the big fin at the back. It really is a hell of a car, he thinks. He'll have a hard time coming up with something that is more fun to drive than this.

He is about to unlock the door when he sees Chuck Corlew appear from the shadows. The gun is in his hand again like it had been in his hand last night, but this time Jack is not so far away. This time the Eldorado isn't going to take a bullet for him.

"Son of a bitch," Chuck says.

He fires three shots and doesn't miss once. Jack looks at Ray on the other side of the Caddy, but it is too late now to say anything.

~~~~~

He doesn't know how long he's stood beside the Cadillac waiting for the stranger with the gun to shoot him too, but he isn't aware of taking any steps and moving away until he hears the sirens in the distance and he realizes the man with the gun is gone and he is standing all alone locked in some kind of screamless dream. He walks around the front of the car hoping not to see what he knows is on the driver's side on the asphalt, but there is Uncle Jack just like he doesn't want him to be there, and Ray stands looking over him wondering if this is going to be the first dead man he is ever going to witness becoming that way. The way Uncle Jack is positioned by the front wheel makes it difficult to tell if he is breathing or not, if he is alive or dead. Gone for good, Ray thinks. He wonders if he is supposed to bend over and find out the answer before anyone gets here or if he is supposed to wait and not touch anything and destroy evidence or any of that stuff he sees on the cop shows on TV. He stands looking at his uncle waiting for an answer.

First there is one police car and then they begin multiplying. A different sort of high frequency siren sounds in his ears and ambulance drivers and paramedics flit back and forth, in and out. Different people ask him questions, looking at him closely as if they are trying to decide if it has been him who had done this terrible thing. He tells them about the stranger with the gun and wonders if they believed him or not or if they think he is making things up and soon they'll get the truth out of him one way or the other. He tells them who he is and who his uncle was. They look at him like he isn't telling them enough, like he knows more about what has happened but isn't letting them in on the real truth. He tells them who his parents are and what their telephone number is while he watches them load Uncle Jack on a stretcher and take him away. There are tubes and wires connected to machines and gadgets and pumps, and he notices how nobody covers his uncle's face with a sheet when they carry him off. He thinks maybe that is a good thing. He wonders why the stranger didn't shoot him too and why he isn't getting carried off with Uncle Jack. He spends a minute or so thinking about how it could have been that he might be dead right this minute and how that would be it for his life. He is amazed at how things come and go and change just like that. All this time he's believed time was forever.

He keeps thinking that soon he is going to be arrested and they will put him in the back of a squad car and take him off to jail, but he keeps standing by the Cadillac answering questions from different people while chalk gets drawn on the pavement and the car door gets dusted and a guy takes about twenty flash pictures with a camera he has to balance on his shoulder like a bazooka. Ray forgets all about how deliciously intoxicated he had been an hour ago and wonders how it is he can be so sober so quickly, and that is when he feels teardrops in his eyes and he wonders why it had taken so long for them to get there and then they are gone and he is empty. He sees his dad and mom coming toward him and he wonders if he knows exactly what to say. He doesn't find that thought too strange at all since it is the way he's been feeling about talking with them for a good while now.

"Ray," Loretta says, "are you all right?" She throws her arms around him and holds him tight, and he stands there and lets her embrace him and does his best not to feel so awkward about her touching him like this. He looks over her shoulder at his dad, who has an expression on his face that looks like it is half sad and the other half is irritated. He's been at work all day, Ray thinks. On Friday nights he likes to go out and eat and then come home and watch television. He's not going to get to do that tonight.

"I can't believe it," Loretta murmurs, letting go of Ray and backing away some. "Poor Jack. He's in bad shape, they say. We've got to go to the hospital right away."

"You're going to have to tell us what happened," Albert says. "I don't know what the two of you were doing down here at night like this."

"Uncle Jack took me to the Friday Night Opry." Ray looks out at the street where the traffic is going by like nothing is wrong. "I saw Jeannie Seely and Jack Greene." He smiles at his parents apologetically. "I never liked country music before."

"Do you need my son for anything else?" Albert asks a man in a suit who looks like he is in charge.

"He can go right now. We'll be calling him, maybe tonight, maybe tomorrow. If we catch the guy we're going to need him to identify him for us."

Ray follows his parents out of the lot and down the walk a few yards to where an assortment of cars block off a side street. Ray doesn't much want to go to the hospital with his parents. He wants to tell them to take him home first so he can go to his room and be alone and lie in bed and look at the ceiling with the lights off so that all he can see are the shadows that come from the porch light and the streetlight out on the road by the mailbox. He thinks that maybe if he is alone and in the dark with nothing poking at his eyes and ears he can think a little and come to some understanding about what has happened and why it is that this is Good Friday and how it is not so good in any way and why it is he is not dead or dying like Uncle Jack is dead or dying right now. He is ashamed of himself for not wanting to go to the hospital to be with his uncle when maybe he is fixing to die and there won't be a chance to be with him again, but the thing is, Ray confesses to himself, he is scared of what he has seen and more scared of what might have been. He has spent all this time for a good long while now wondering about this world he is living in and never given the first thought about how the world was here before him and was still going to be around when he wasn't.

He doesn't know how to keep it in his head. He has never thought about how everything will go on even if he isn't around. It has never occurred to him at all.

~~~~~

They come home from the hospital after midnight. Loretta wants to get some things together so she can go back in the morning after getting a little sleep, and so Ray walks down the hall to his bedroom to get some sleep too. Brenda is gone for the night but there is a light on in John's room. Ray starts to knock on the door and tell him what has happened but he keeps on going. He doesn't see much use in talking to his brother. It isn't like there is anything he can tell him. John can find out everything from Loretta and Albert later.

They are home maybe an hour when the phone rings and he hears his mother crying. He starts to get up and let her tell him Uncle Jack is dead, but dead is a permanent thing and Ray decides she can tell him in the morning and it won't make that much difference. He tries to get comfortable and let his mind go blank while he looks out the window to where the light from the street is edging along the glass. There is a lot of stuff in his mind but he is trying not to listen to it for a while.

There will be plenty of time for that later.

~~~~~

On Saturday Loretta and Albert go to the hospital early to release Jack's body and make funeral arrangements. Ray doesn't go with them because he has to go down to City Hall and make a statement for the police. He doesn't know what else he can tell them he hasn't told them Friday night, but he makes the trip down to City Hall anyway feeling glad he has something else to do besides think. He is having a lot of trouble letting things sink in.

On the ride in he turns off the radio and drives along in silence. It is a pretty day with the sun shining and the world in bloom, and there are times as he drives along he forgets what he is doing and where he is going just looking at the colors and feeling the warm breeze coming in the window and refreshing him all over. Soon there will be no need for sweaters and jackets and long sleeves. Soon it will be spring all the time and the frost will be gone and the winds will be warm and school will be close to letting out for the summer. And when he comes back in the fall he will be a senior.

He tries to stop himself from thinking it, but it comes through his mind loud and clear anyway. It is a good thing he's already had his senior gift from Uncle Jack. He is driving this car right now courtesy of him. If Uncle Jack hadn't bought this car for him this week he wouldn't have been around to do it next year. Ray doesn't like to think like this but it is still the truth. For some reason all of this had happened this way, like the stars were aligned or something. It is like there is a pattern and a plan for everything and no matter what a guy does it is all going to come into being anyway. He decides maybe if he tells himself crap like this about a hundred times then maybe he won't feel so bad about things after a while. Maybe he'll really believe in his heart that Uncle Jack was going to die anyway and that he and his 1963 Chevrolet Super Sport didn't have anything to do with it.

He doesn't have to stay long at the police station. During the night, the detective working the case tells him, they'd caught the guy who'd shot Uncle Jack. One of Jack's friends knew who the guy was and what the shooting had been about, and all they had to do was go and talk to the woman and she had told them right where her ex-husband was living. He was waiting for us when we got there, the detective says. He knew we'd show up fairly soon. You'll have to testify as a witness at his trial, Ray is told, unless he pleads guilty early and there isn't a trial. Lots of guys will do that if they know there's no hope for them just so they can go to prison for life and not go to the electric chair. Nobody wants to fry.

It is close to noon and Ray is hungry. He starts to go to the Burger Chef to get a sandwich, but when he drives by he sees Ann's car parked in front, so he doesn't stop. He doesn't want to talk to her today, maybe not for the rest of his life. He isn't sure if the news about his uncle is out yet, but he doesn't want to have to explain anything to anyone if it is, and besides, he can't get the image of how Ann Caldwell had looked the other night out of his head. How could he talk to her after that? How could he desire her in the least? He feels himself slipping away from any kind of involvement in what is supposed to be his life. He doesn't know how to put his finger on it, but there is something in him that says he needs to move on. Maybe he isn't in the position to be able to do it physically, but it is up there in his mind, and that is a start. Like the flowers and the wild onions of spring, he knows that idea is going to do nothing but grow over the next days and weeks and months of his life. He is not going to be happy in this place. He is going to have to leave it behind. He doesn't know if doing that will make him happy or not, if it will fix things in him whatsoever, but it will be a start. He will have to try.

Before it dawns on him too clearly he finds himself on the bridge crossing the Cumberland River into downtown Nashville. He supposes he has meant to end up here all along, but he hasn't been able to focus on anything as a direct plan all the way in, but has instead just felt himself floating and drifting with the wind and allowing it to carry him somewhere where he could make some sense of what happened last night before his eyes but which he hasn't been able to yet see in any kind of clarity. He thinks perhaps retracing his steps from last night might bring him closer to some form of acceptance. He is going to have to do it soon, so it might as well be now. He can't spend Easter weekend waiting for Uncle Jack's funeral with his family around him watching and waiting for him to tell them why something like last night had happened. Perhaps it isn't true, but he still feels himself responsible for it in some way. Even if he gets it to a point where he can let himself off the hook as the cause of Uncle Jack's death, he still won't be able to shake the feeling that everybody in his family believes it has happened because of him.

There is the Krystal on Church Street just up from the movie houses, so he swings his car into one of the vacant lots and walks up the sidewalk to go inside. The place is crowded with people shopping downtown for the Easter holiday, dresses and hats and suits and such, and Ray has to wait a minute for a stool at the counter to come open. He orders his burgers from the waitress and looks at himself and the shoppers milling around him in the big mirror that runs across the wall. He can see his own image in the glass before him, but he still has trouble distinguishing himself from the others around him. It is like he is different now, a stranger to himself whom he has not seen before. Maybe it has taken this long to pick himself out from the throng because the guy he has grown so used to seeing before is not here with him today. That guy is gone, Ray thinks. I am going to have to get used to the fact that I am a different person now. I am not the same anymore.

He finishes and walks out and down the sidewalk where all the department stores are open with people going in and out the doors and crossing the intersections when the lights change. In the display windows perfect female mannequins pose in new dresses beside handsome counterparts in suits and perfect plastic children in pink and blue and red dresses, white sport coats with bow ties and hair that is never mussed. All the figures smile and point with their fingers at something Ray can't see—the sunshine, a puppy, the Easter Bunny hopping down the bunny trail. Just off in the corner stands the Easter Bunny himself, holding a basket with eggs and grass and candy. Ray tries to remember when his mother stopped making him a basket every year. He had been just a little guy when that happened. She gathered him and John and Brenda together and told them the Easter Bunny wasn't going to come anymore. Easter isn't about candy, she had said. I would rather you spend Easter day thinking about Jesus and how he died for your sins on the cross. I want you to think about how he rose from the grave. I want you to think about how he said, forgive them, for they know not what they do.

He finds the lot where Uncle Jack had been shot and there isn't anything about it that looks familiar. No flashing lights are around, no yellow police tape stretches across the scene of the crime, no detectives with memo pads or photographers taking flash pictures. The Eldorado is gone too, towed off to be dusted and used as evidence when the time comes for a trial. And after that, who knows what would happen to it? Ray wonders if it will go to his mother, since she is Jack's closest next of kin. He imagines the sight of Loretta driving the Cadillac down Main Street to a church service, and the idea of it is so preposterous that he sweeps it from his mind immediately. No, his mother would never do anything like that. Nor would Albert. Ray knows that for a fact. Uncle Jack's car would never be allowed as a part of their family unit, because it is a symbol of wildness and sin, of what was wrong with a life that was apart from God and Heaven, and a reminder of how when a person chooses to pursue a life with no spiritual buoy then ruin and decay and death are sure to happen. The wages of sin cannot be far behind. The Cadillac could never be brought near for fear it contained some kind of spiritual poison oak. It would infect and spread and engulf with its history whoever came near. It is a thing of evil, a foretaste of Satan and wickedness. It will have to be cast off and thrown away, never to be looked at or thought about again. It is not a Ford.

So there is nothing to see. Ray stands for a moment looking at the parked cars that know nothing of last night's history and the asphalt that bears no traces of blood, and then he walks back to his car through the shoppers filling the crosswalks and the walkways. He can hear their voices as he passes but he doesn't understand a word of what they have to say.

He can't stand the thought of going home, so he drives to the motel where his uncle had stayed the past six days to see if there is anything he can find of understanding there, but he doesn't stop because his father's Fairlane is parked in a slot by the room. He guesses his mother and father are inside gathering up the remainder of Jack's belongings and bringing them back to the house—his razor and shaving cream, deodorant, toothpaste and toothbrush. Maybe there is a suitcase or two, shirts and pants and socks and underwear, a sport coat and a few ties. Probably there is a bottle of whiskey sitting around, but Ray already knows they will leave that behind. His mother would throw it in the trash, and they would tell everybody from this day on how it had been the whiskey and the denial of his Heavenly Father that had really been the reason Jack had died. The bullets that lodged in him were only the result of the road he had traveled to be where he met his fate. Ray doesn't know how many times he can listen to such a tale. He has not heard it yet—he has only imagined it in his head—but he is sick of it already.

When he gets back to the Super Sport he already knows he can't go back home until he's seen the Cadillac one more time. He drives across the bridge toward the east side of the river and sees the tall chain fence surrounding the hundreds of cars parked behind them with whitewashed numbers on their windshields. Somewhere in there is Uncle Jack's Eldorado, and he parks and walks back and forth trying to pick out a flash of cherry red that will reveal its location. It is Saturday, though, and the lot is closed and the gates are locked. Probably a car such as his uncle's is parked far inside the lot, surrounded by other tow-ins and wrecks and repossessions like guards against plunderers who might attempt to move it, to steal it, to take it away. Ray can see it is basically useless for him to try and find the Eldorado. There has been no provision made for one such as him to come here and say goodbye to it, for that isn't the way anyone in the real world acts these days. Only Ray would think to come down here to bid adieu to a red Cadillac Eldorado, like it is a lover or a friend in some way. No one else, he is sure, would attempt anything so damned stupid.

Saturday night stretches before him like an unknown highway. He thinks of his mother and father coming home from the motel with the car trunk loaded with what had been Uncle Jack's possessions, and Ray visualizes Loretta and Albert at dinner tonight, talking of what they have found and explaining it to Brenda, expounding on the rules and regulations of life with John, and all the time shooting questioning glances and looks Ray's way, as if they expect an explanation of why Jack had chosen him, of why it was that their middle son was the one who had been by his side like a compatriot when he died. Ray wonders how long they will wait to get an answer from him, and, if he takes too long to let them know, how long it will be before they give up on him too and resign themselves to the fact that he is only another Jack Patterson in the making, and that nothing good is ever going to come of him either.

He knows before he starts scaling the chain-link fence that he isn't going to go home. He isn't going to be at any such dinner tonight. He isn't going to sit under everyone's gaze and play the black sheep of the family role, and he isn't going to have everyone whispering under their breath how he is nothing but a Jack Patterson Junior. No, fuck that. He'll let them have those precious little moments all to themselves. He won't be around to have to sit and take it, like he is some little kid and it is time he learned a lesson or two.

So he climbs the fence to get to the other side. He could be arrested for this. Trespassing, he thinks, and it seems real funny at the moment. He could also kill himself if he falls, he tells himself, so be careful. This seems funny to him too.

There doesn't seem to be any alarm system that is going to bring the cops right away. There is no guard dog with teeth or even a watchman anywhere about that he can see, so he takes his time going up and down the rows of cars looking for the Cadillac. Most of the cars are dark and wrecked and covered with grime, so it doesn't take eagle's vision on his part to spot the bright shiny candy red of the Eldorado when he comes to the end of the first section of cars.

It is parked by a shed that has a front porch with a railing. The building looks like it houses an office of some kind, and Ray deduces this is where someone has to go to when they pay a towing fee or have to fork out when their car has been stored for a while. The door is shut and a shade is pulled down over the solitary window, so Ray knows no one is around to bother him right now. Probably he shouldn't hang around too long, but he doesn't have to really hurry either.

He hopes the Cadillac isn't locked because that would complicate matters if it is. He tries the handle and the driver's door opens, and he slides into the seat and puts his hands on the wheel. He wishes the top was down but he doesn't have time to mess with it now. He spends a minute looking out the windshield and moving the wheel, turning switches and knobs and punching the radio selector buttons. There is no engine roar, no country music from the radio, but he still feels the majesty and power of the car. Uncle Jack had loved this car, just like he had instinctively known that Ray would love the Super Sport. It was like an unspoken thing the two of them both understood. They understood because in many ways they were from the same place. Ray knows this minute no one else in his family has any idea where this place is. They have never been there and they would never go.

There is nothing in the glove compartment to keep as a memento of Uncle Jack; the bottle of Jack Daniel's that was there last night is gone. There are no papers or swizzle sticks or anything that might have provided a clue as to who this gleaming piece of metal had once belonged to. It is almost like Uncle Jack had never driven it down a highway.

Maybe that's the way it is, Ray thinks. Maybe in the end the world likes to wipe everything you touched once spotless and act like you were never really around. It cleans up the mess you left behind and makes it look like none of it ever happened in the first place.

Ray sits for a while with his hands on the wheel. Before he gets out he sounds the horn a good long blast. What the fuck, he thinks.

~~~~~

He doesn't go home. He passes right by his street along the way and stops at the Burger Chef for a cheeseburger and French fries, sitting in his usual booth and looking out at his car in the lot. The way the sun's rays are hitting it makes it look brand new. It is hard to believe it is almost five years old, just like it is hard to believe he will be eighteen in a few months.

He doesn't know if he is waiting for Jimmy or Ann Caldwell and her friends or somebody else to show up. He doesn't think so. He is just sitting, waiting for the sun to go down. He is having an early supper here, because the mood he is in right now he believes he's had his last supper at home. Sure, he'll be there to eat plenty more times in the flesh, but what he is feeling now is something else. It has a lot to do with his mind.

In his head he isn't going to be around for too much anymore.

He drives to the motel and parks in their lot, then hikes past the Lutheran church and begins climbing the hill. In his right hand he carries the quarter-full bottle of whiskey, holding it tightly so there is no danger of dropping it. He wants to make sure it gets to the top of the hill with him safely, just so he and the remaining dregs of Jack Daniel's his uncle has introduced him to can sit on the mound overlooking the highway and watch the cars go back and forth, on their way into Nashville or coming from it on the way back home to somewhere, Goodlettsville, Springfield, Clarksville—it is hard to tell where people are coming from or going to. All he can really determine is they are headed somewhere.

Like he is.

It will be a while before he can go. He knows that already. He will have to do a lot of waiting and being patient, keeping his mouth closed when he has something to say, taking notice of what is happening around him so he won't get caught up in anything that might cause a delay. He can't make any kind of announcement of his intentions, because he has seen how it goes on that, how people tend to act. They all want to stop you. They want to make you stay.

But he is going. There isn't any doubt about that.

The day is coming where nothing can hold him. He'll nod his head and smile and get in his bright red Super Sport and drive off and somehow no one will be able to tell much of a difference of his being around or gone for good. He knows he's been gone already for a long time anyway. It's just nobody has seen him go because they haven't been looking. They haven't been paying attention. It's the way things have been for quite a while.

Super Sport

ABOUT RALPH BLAND

Ralph Bland grew up in East Nashville and received a smidgen of education from the Metro Nashville School System, namely Rosebank Elementary and Stratford High School, although both institutions deny having any affiliation with him. He is a 1973 graduate of Belmont University, where he majored in English and spent most semesters on Chapel Probation. He spent 38 years with the Kroger Company before being run off in 2005 to spend a few hectic years delivering snacks and sodas to ungrateful clients. He returned then to the grocery business as a manager/bookkeeper at one of the last independent stores in Nashville and retired in August, 2012, to devote time to his writing, his three dogs, and his wonderful wife, who with this prospect in mind decided to pick up her workload with Metropolitan Nashville Public Schools.

His first novel, ONCE IN LOVE WITH AMY, appeared in 2002, followed by WHERE OR WHEN (2004) and PAST PERFECT (2006). A collection of previously published short stories, NOT DEAD AGAIN: STORIES BY RALPH BLAND, appeared in 2011. ACE was released in May of 2012, LONG LONG TIME in April 2014, and his current release, BRIGHT RED DEVIL, in November 2014.

When not coercing himself to write he likes to spend his time suffering over the misfortunes of his beloved Vanderbilt Commodores Mens' basketball team, lounging with his spoiled dogs, or tinkering with his 1949 Wurlitzer jukebox in vain attempts to determine why one day it works and the next day it doesn't, knowing full well that because he is a mechanical idiot he will never arrive at the answer. A lover of Universal Monster movies and British sports cars that don't run, he is the proud owner of perhaps Tennessee's largest Frank Sinatra collection, as if that has anything to do with the price of tea in China. Visit his website at http://www.ralphbland.com